TATTOOED TRAUMA

MIRACAL MARTIN

CONTENTS

"*T*ake your shirt off." Skully stated.

"Damn straight to it." He chuckled, extending his hand. "I'm Law."

"Hm. I'm Skully and I didn't ask. But now that the pleasantries are out the way..." Skully started.

"Why do they call you Skully?" He inquired.

"Why do they call you Law?" She challenged. "Let me guess because you're always breaking it." She said mockingly. "Corny street name, for a corny nigga?"

He laughed it off, not taking offense.

"Nah." He shook his head. "It's because I'm in Law School and maybe something to do with the fact that my mother named me Lawrence."

"Hmph." She grinned, running her tongue along her cheek. She had read that all wrong but remained unapologetic about it. "That makes more sense I guess."

"Your turn."

"Nope. Your turn still." Like everyone, he assumed she'd given him her nickname. It wasn't surprising. "They call me Skully because that's my name. I don't do nicknames."

"I like it. It works for you."

"I'll bet. Listen, you're my first client of the day. Far from last. Got to get this show on the road, honey." She clasped her hands together.

"No problem. I just thought I'd introduce myself, seeing as how you got me feeling like a trick."

"Feel how you want, just feel it with your shirt off." Skully retorted. "I'll take my money now too."

"Damn, I have to pay upfront? What if I'm not pleased with your service?"

"Read the sign."

Behind her in all red letters, all caps 'CASH ONLY, UPFRONT, NO REFUND!'

"So, what's up we doing this or what?" She arched an eyebrow, slowly losing patience.

"You come highly recommended." He slid his shirt over his head in one motion.

He had a body that her eyes could appreciate.

Looked like he should be on the football field somewhere. Big strong arms, nice big hands. He towered over her 5 ft 6 frame, had to be at least 6 ft 2 give or take an inch.

He pulled his wallet from his pocket, peeling off 5-hundred-dollar bills.

"Thank you." She walked over to place the money in

a drawer. She needed to get her eyes off him. At least for a second to return her thoughts from the lustful daydream they had gone into, back to professionalism.

He could appreciate the view. Skully had just enough of everything to him. Slim waist, hips for days, and an ample ass that sat up just right. It wasn't the biggest, but perfect for her frame.

"Have a seat. Lay back." She instructed.

He obliged, watching her prepare herself.

She pulled her hair into a bun. Then pulled herself a chair, adjusting it for her comfort.

"It's clearly not either of ours first time," She glanced over his defined, tattoo-covered chest. She took a minute to admire it. "I don't know your tolerance for pain, but you know… it comes with pleasure." She shrugged, "I pride myself on customer satisfaction so hopefully this will be a good experience for us both.

"I'm sure it will."

Looking up at her face, there were a lot of things he'd let her do to him at that moment, regardless of the consequences.

"Do you mind music?"

"Whatever works for you."

"Good. I don't work without it ever. Just thought I'd ask for the hell of it."

He could only shake his head. She was funny to him.

Something about the needle in her hand and the

hum as the machine came to life, gave Skully an adrenaline rush.

He didn't even flinch as the needle touched his skin.

He closed his eyes as his muscles relaxed like it was as tranquil as it could get. They were both mutually in their own personal heaven.

"So, how long have you been doing this?" He questioned. "Tattooing?"

"You're talking to me?" Skully remarked.

"Who else?" He challenged.

"Yeah uh... don't do that," Skully replied. "That's what the music's for."

A long silence rest as she got lost in the world of ink.

Portrait tattoos were her absolute favorite.

As tedious as they were, they had the ability to both keep her up at night and make her feel warm inside. From the perfectionist in her studying every detail. Then the satisfying feeling that came with a job well done.

Skully had studied the picture for hours, from the slight gap between her two front teeth, to her dimpled right cheek.

Skully had every intention to execute the tattoo with passion and precision.

Skully cleared her throat breaking the silence she had demanded. "Who is she?"

"Hm... Look who's talking." He smirked. He didn't answer immediately.

It would have been perfectly fine if he didn't answer at all. Skully dished out plenty, she could take it when people gave her a dose of her own medicine.

"My sister." He answered.

"She's beautiful." Skully complimented. "Y'all must be close."

"She's very beautiful." He agreed. "We were."

The use of past tense made her feel unsettled. Judging by the increased rise and fall of his chest she wasn't alone.

"Hey! Chill out all that breathing." She teased hoping to lighten the mood.

He chuckled in response.

Just like that, they were back in their own worlds.

---

4 ½ hours later she was rubbing a layer of petroleum jelly along the tattoo and bandaging it for him.

He had already analyzed it for about five minutes, complimenting her ability to articulate every single last detail.

"I don't even think you realize just how much this means to me." His smile was perfection, his eyes revealed the authenticity behind it. "Thank you. They said you were the best and you lived up to it"

"No, thank you. I'm glad you're happy with it." The tips of her fingers were still on his chocolate-dipped arms.

Their work with each other was done, yet he lingered. So did she, it was now her turn to admire the work of art that was Law.

"Well, um…" She cleared her throat. "I have to get cleaned up for my next client."

"Uh yeah. Let me get out of your way." He pulled his shirt back over his head. Followed by his jacket.

Skully was already busying herself wiping down the chair.

"Was there something else?" She placed a hand on her hip.

From his broad shoulders, thick brows, and the height that towered over her.

When their eyes locked, she quickly averted eye contact.

He shook his head. "Thanks again." He lifted a hand to her on his way out.

———

"Look who the wind blew in…" Storm greeted her.

"Oh, the dramatics." Skully rolled her eyes. "It's been all of two days."

"It's been three." Storm corrected her. "And it

wouldn't be so bad if you answered the phone or responded to text like normal people. I just like to know that my sister's alive, ya know?"

It was true Skully was a terrible communicator. Not intentionally.

She knew her twin sister Storm was needy, but sometimes she just needed her own space.

Her phone spent more time on DND than anything, because in most instances she did not need to be disturbed.

"Well, you never know when the wind will blow me in next, so why not just feed me and make me happy now." She was already following her into the kitchen.

Where her niece Jelani, Nari, and Torrian were. Torrian was Storm's husband's brother and Nari was his girlfriend.

One thing about Storm's house, it felt like home to everyone. It was fitting because Storm loved to play host. The doors were always welcomed to their friends and family and it was like neutral ground for them all.

"Hey y'all." Skully greeted them.

"Hey, Jelani boo." She greeted her niece who sat at the dining room table coloring away. They did their handshake which ended in a hand explosion.

"Where's Bren?" Skully asked.

"Girl," Storm rolled her eyes half-heartedly. "Don't talk him up."

"Jelani, go ahead and put that coloring book away doll." Storm told her. "Go wash your hands."

Skully could see the tiniest bit of hesitation come over her face before she quickly came to her senses and obliged.

"What's on the menu?" Skully washed her hands and retrieved a glass and plate from the cabinet.

"Noodles & gizzards, sweet peas, and cornbread."

"Now you know my niece don't like no damn peas. Get your life."

"Let her tell it she's allergic to anything green honey, I'm not hearing it."

"Yeah well, what happened to your diet? This time last week you were only eating salads and drinking smoothies."

"Girl, a salad don't do shit for me but sit it my stomach and wait for the real food to join the party."

Skully cracked up laughing while preparing her plate.

"You don't need to be losing weight anyway," Nari added her two cents.

It was true.

"I'm packing a little extra around this belly girl. I been hella bloated."

When Storm entered the dining room with Jelani's plate, she had already set her tablet up, her new obsession being Youtube.

"Jelani cut it out. Take that tablet to your room." Storm shook her head.

"I know she be cussing you all out in her head."

"She better keep it in her head. That's her second tablet."

"I smell that good food, and I see my little princess!" Brennon scooped Jelani up just as she was heading back into the dining room.

"Daddy put me down." Jelani giggled hysterically.

"What up sis?" He nudged Skully just as he was putting Jelani to her feet. "Kiddos." That had been how he referred to his brother for the longest, Nari got added in by default in the few years she'd been around.

Their 7-year difference meant Brennon, and Torrian were always at two different stages in their lives. Still, they had always been relatively close.

"Hey baby." He gave Storm a brief shoulder massage.

"Babe, did you get my Mega Millions?"

"I knew I was forgetting something."

"Now why would you bring your raggedy-ass in here without my Mega?" She kissed her teeth.

"Calm your crazy ass down girl," he chuckled. "I got all five of your Mega Millions." He made the five tickets rain on her.

Torrian shook his head. He said it time and time and he'd say it again- his brother was forever simping.

"Good, cause I'm feeling lucky." Storm smiled rubbing her hands together.

"Girl." Skully couldn't help but laugh at her sister's antics.

She passed her the wine glass when she got up to go make Brennon's plate. "Wine me please."

This was like her little family.

At 26 and 27- years old, they'd been together 11 years, married 5, with a 6-year-old daughter Jelani.

Storm and Brennon were like that young-old couple that made marriage seem dope.

The next day, Skully spent the entire day at the tattoo shop. She barely even had a break in between work. Now, as she cleaned her room, she already had one foot out the door.

"Hi baby," Koda greeted her.

That was Koda, everyone was "baby".

Koda had been in the shop going on two years, when she came walking in the shop about six months later than her it was natural for their male-dominated environment to attempt pitting them against each other. Emphasis on attempt.

Koda was sweet as pie and Skully had no interest in beefing with other women, other black women especially.

"Hey boo." Skully was sitting in her chair, relaxing before her next client.

The way the shop was set up, they all rented out their own rooms and hardly ever had to see each other.

However, the shop was typically good vibes, and they all got along well.

"I know you like your uninterrupted alone time, but I just wanted to make sure you knew about Lee's surprise 70's themed birthday party." Koda said.

"Fool bout to be drunk as all get out." Skully shook her head. "Lord knows he don't need a party for that."

"That is a fact. So yeah, I hope you'll come. I'm sure you could use some fun in your life, among other things." She grinned.

Skully rolled her eyes, "Oh whatever."

"For real, it's gon be a good time. Extend the invite to Storm too, I know he'll want her there too."

Before marriage, and Jelani Lee was Storm's turn-up buddies. The two of them together was always trouble.

"Should we wait for Skully?" Camile asked.

"Now you know damn well she's not coming." Storm responded. "Get the waitress back over here so we can get some drinks going, cause honey I need one or two."

Besides her sister, her very-first best friend Storm had her best friend Kaice, and Brennon's cousin Jeremiah's fiancé, who had been in the family for years.

Then there was of course Nari, the youngin. It was a big sister, little sister relationship between them.

"Well, let me take those shots with you." Camile shook her head. "Because now that I got this ring, Wilma swears I'm about to start popping out children."

"Well… isn't that what they say?" Kaice replied. "First comes love, then comes marriage, then comes the…"

"Fuck they! I don't know who the hell they are, but they, like Wilma, can stay out of my uterus."

"Say that, say that!" Kaice replied. "All jokes aside, I do think it's ridiculous the pressure put on women. Like… I don't have to be married by thirty. I don't have to have kids if that's not something I want, and if it is, that's still not something for you to inquire."

"Exactly! With that being said…" Camile began. "After the wedding, and honeymoon and all the fun stuff is out the way I'm going to get off the birth control."

"Okay! Big news."

"I'm excited. I mean I think we're established. We've moved into our forever home, and I'm not putting any pressure on it. I'm just getting off this birth control and letting the Lord do his work. When it's time, it's time."

"Yes. Start popping out them children!" Storm nodded her head. "My baby needs some friends."

"You know what's crazy, I've never been on birth control." Nari announced.

"What?!?"

"Listen… One thing about Shanice, she put the fear of God in me about having a baby before I was equipped to care for it. She always told me to come to her when I was ready to be on birth control but after I did my research, I was like to hell with it!"

"Don't tell me you and Torrian's only form of protection is the pull-out method."

"Pull out, condom… whatever it takes. I'm just not going to bear all the responsibility. I'm not going to subject myself to something so taxing on my body, just because you don't like condoms. Either you take responsibility to keep babies from happening or you get ready to go half on them responsibilities."

"Whew. That's a lot of responsibility you're placing in Torrian's hands." Storm commented.

"Hey! My man's more responsible than you give him credit for." Nari defended him. "3-years in… no babies."

"No pregnancy scares?" Storm crossed her arms arching her eyebrows.

"Mind your business." Nari pointed.

"Alright enough of all of this. Go talk to y'all gyno, not me!" Kaice replied. "But… we can all take shots for Camile's uterus and all ten of her offspring's because Jeremiah ain't ever pulling out." She stuck her tongue out waving over their waitress.

"What up cuz?" Law greeted his cousin Lee, followed by his brother Terrance who he dapped up. "Big bruh."

"I can't call it," Lee responded. "You smoking?"

"Now you know…" Law gave him a look.

"Just checking," Lee smirked.

"Let me go in here and speak. I'll be back." Law stated entering the house. "Hey ma." Law greeted her with a kiss on the cheek. "What's up Larry?" Law had a good relationship with his stepfather.

Growing up, Law, Terrance, and Amira had been more than happy to see their parents break up. None of them harbored any ill feelings. In fact, Law couldn't ever recall seeing his mother as happy with his father as she was with Larry.

"How you been youngin?" Larry asked.

"Exhausted. Everything's coming together for me though." Law answered. "It hasn't been easy, but you know nothing worth it ever is."

"You can say that again, but it's in you not on you. You're almost to the finish line."

"Preciate that Larry." He turned his attention to his mother. "How much longer on the food?"

"About 30-40 minutes."

"Bet." He stepped back onto the porch.

"I meant to ask what's up with ole girl?" Law asked.

"It would behoove you to be a lil more specific my nigga." Lee replied. "You could be talking about hella girls."

"Yeah, but you know who I'm talking about."

"Yeah, and you know her name."

"Skully."

"What about her?"

"I know you not sitting here acting like you trying to get at somebody..." Terrance shook his head. "You can't even get your old bitch under control."

"Aye, watch that," Law warned. "Me and Tatum aren't even together right now."

"Exactly. Not right now."

"Nah for real, if you don't have that other situation under control there's no point in even stepping to Skully," Lee stated.

"Lee, you sound like you got something going with ole girl." Terrance accused. "That some of your old work?"

"Not at all. She works for me. You know me better than that." Lee answered honestly. "I got a lot of love for her though, and she's been through her fair of shit. I linked you with one of my dope artists. I wasn't playing matchmaker. Don't even try it with her."

Everything Lee was saying was going in one ear and out the other.

Skully had perked Law's interest and if the opportunity presented itself, he had every intention of going for it.

2

"*H*ey boo." Nari greeted Torrian as he entered the house. "How was work?"

"Work." He sighed walking over to give her a quick kiss. "Hey mama." He gave her a kiss on the cheek.

"Hey handsome," Shanice replied.

He and Shanice had a wonderful relationship, a blessing, and a curse. It annoyed Nari how Shanice would be on Torrian's side at times.

"Sorry, we turned the living room into a salon." Nari apologized. "Shanice just came over begging to play in my head."

"The lies you tell." Shanice shook her head. "Go ahead and send me my cash app too. $Moneymaking-milf. I'm not playing with you."

They all laughed at that. Shanice was a true mess.

"Just off the strength of that being your cashapp name, I'm not sending you anything."

"Play if you want. Bet you be looking crazy. Weave halfway sewn in."

"I got you ma." Torrian spoke up. "That's probably what it was gon come to anyway."

"See that's my son right there!" Shanice boasted. "Go head in that kitchen, I brought you some corned beef, red potatoes, macaroni, and cornbread."

"Why you have to go crazy like that?" He stepped back dramatically. "I knew you loved me!"

"Boy calm down. Acting like I don't keep you well-fed."

"Well… it's that well part that we still working on."

Nari gave him the middle finger.

"Let me go get in on this plate." He rubbed his hands together.

"Babe, Destiny's here by the way!" Nari called after him, warning him so that her presence didn't surprise him.

Torrian entered the kitchen where Destiny was making a plate of her own. "Destiny." He addressed her friend, who glared in his direction.

Just evil. Whenever she addressed him it was always with an attitude so he made no effort to be polite to her in return.

"Torrian." She replied dryly. "Hope you're not too hungry, I took the last of the corned beef." She flashed him a fake smile.

Torrian muttered something under his breath that

18

she didn't catch. "What was that?" she turned back towards him.

"Nothing."

"Now I know you hear me knocking, yet you act like you don't." After knocking several times, Skully tried her luck and fortunately, the door was unlocked.

"That's literally the definition of ignoring someone." Her roommate/ ex-friend Ebony responded.

It'd gone from helping a friend who fell on hard times for a couple of months, then 4, then 7. By 9 months Skully felt it was only right that Ebony be contributing to the household. That's when shit went left field. Over a year and a half later, Skully had the roommate from hell. There wasn't much time left on the lease, to begin with, Skully was counting down the days.

"Well, I hope you don't think you're ignoring that rent that's due."

She was grateful this was her last time having to come in collect. She could've easily spazzed on Ebony, but she kept their interactions to a minimum because it wasn't worth wasting her energy.

"Already slid it under your door."

That was a shock.

"You should probably start packing up, too. Can't

just leave it any kind of way," the latter of her statement was mumbled on her way out of the door.

"You should probably kiss my ass." Ebony muttered.

"Say that again." Skully turned back.

"Can you close my door?" Ebony rolled her eyes.

Skully fought against being childish and slamming the door. It wouldn't even be half as satisfying as slamming Ebony's head against it.

"Now where the hell you think you going?" Brennon was not pleased. His furrowed eyebrows bore genuine confusion.

"I told you about Lee's party." Storm said innocently.

Storm was dressed in a gold metallic catsuit with a keyhole opening in the front, crisscross halter straps that tied in the back, bellbottom legs, and a gold round belt.

She picked her hair out and let it do its thing around her head.

Storm crossed the room eyes searching for her clutch,

It was all in the body. Her c-cup breast was sitting up just right. Hard nipples just poking out at him.

She lost the stomach, kept the curves, and unfortunately the stretch marks. Stretch marks that Brennon made her love because he loved them and her so much. Brennon was a daily boost for her self-esteem.

"Man for real," He pulled her down onto the bed, hugging her body. "You in for the night. Bye Skully."

"Stop baby." Storm giggled. "We need to head out. I'm not trying to be out super late."

"Super late?!? It's already past wife hours."

"Boy, whatever."

That's one of the things Skully admired about her sister the most. Her ability to be a doting wife and mother, while never losing sight of who she was at the core.

And another thing, she loved about their relationship; Brennon was never going to stop her from enjoying herself.

"Alright, but you gon get somebody killed."

He could joke all he wanted but trying to control Storm just didn't even feel right to Brennon. Beyond that, he genuinely wanted her to enjoy herself he applauded her whenever she did go out.

"Y'all be careful, call me if y'all need me."

———

Lee knew everybody and everybody knew Lee, it came as no surprise the rink was packed.

Lee was too drunk to even be surprised, he just came in dancing like the party had already started in his head.

In any setting Storm was a social butterfly, it was no surprise she and Lee went right into party mode like the old days.

"What the hell you looking at?" Skully snapped.

"Damn you rude." He laughed.

"And you think you're too cool for a costume law school?" She questioned.

"Not at all." He shook his head, taking a sip from his red cup.

She wouldn't have been opposed to it had he said yes. He was cool as a cucumber, smooth as a criminal.

"I wasn't even supposed to be coming tonight, but I got a lil time on my hands. Thought I'd come show some love." He explained. "Hell, my cousin so drunk I don't even think he'll know I was here."

"You're Lee's cousin?"

"First cousin." He confirmed.

Skully wondered why she had only recently met him.

She nodded her head, their eyes locked again as he went for another sip of his drink.

"You look good though." He complimented her.

Skully wore a tie-dye cropped shirt, a pair of flared blue jeans with her hair in two big puffs. She still wore her skates even though she was contemplating calling it a wrap for the night as far as the skating went.

"Thank you." She smiled.

"Well, I heard somewhere you could learn everything you need to know about a man by the way he skates... so... let me see you skate."

"Only if you join me."

"I can't skate."

"I can't either. We'll struggle together."

They both downed their drinks.

Struggle was an understatement.

Everyone around them seemed to be pros. There were whole skate teams doing routines around them.

Skully could barely walk straight with the alcohol flowing through her, much less skate.

"Here, I got you." He held out his hand to her, barely maintaining his own balance.

"You barely got yourself." Skully laughed taking the lead to push herself forward. Just as she did that, he fell right behind her.

Skully felt halfway bad, but her attempt to turn and give him a hand landed her right on the floor with him.

If it weren't for her inebriated state, Skully probably wouldn't be having nearly as much fun. She would feel it in the morning.

She hadn't been skating since she was like 16, she felt like a kid again.

The skates proved to be the worst enemy to the bell-bottoms she wore. At least she was blaming it on that. They kept getting caught under the wheels.

When she realized an hour had passed it felt like it. She'd been laughing her ass off and sweating her hair out.

Storm came around the rink and circled around her, "I'm not sure what I see..." She looked between Skully and Law. "But I see you." She signaled with her hands that she was watching them before skating off.

"A twin? Hm... didn't know that." He rolled up beside her.

"Yeah well, you don't really know me." She stated. "We're strangers."

"We don't have to be that."

"What does that mean?"

"It means, I'd be interested in getting to know you if I thought you'd be interested in letting me."

"I'm not interested."

"Then that's what it is then. I didn't come over here to get you worked up. I just saw a familiar face thought I'd speak. You take care."

He skated off the rink and something about it annoyed the hell out of Skully. She went followed suit but as luck would have it, she fell just as she was about to exit. It was like a chain reaction all 6 people behind her fell as well.

The smirk on Law's face when she looked up at him irritated her soul.

———

"This has got to be the slowest Uber driver in the world, bruh."

It hadn't gotten chilly out, and traffic had accumulated from everyone trying to leave at the same time.

According to the map he'd turned around for the third time.

"Finally." She slapped her hands against her legs as he pulled up in front of them on the sidewalk.

Storm had already tried opening the door before he could even get it unlocked.

"It would've been nice If y'all would've tried to get my attention or something," he was already bitching. "All these people out here." He commented, pulling away.

"What do you call me waving my hand in the air for 30 fucking minutes?" Storm hissed.

"Oh uh-uh." The car came to a stop, and the locks clicked. "We not doing this."

"What?" Storm's face scrunched up in irritation.

"Get out of my car." He stated.

"I know you fucking lying!"

Skully had to shush her sister, while she tried de-escalating the situation that was being blown way out of proportion. "Is that really necessary, I mean…"

"I said, get out of my car. I'm not saying it again."

Just by his demeanor, she read that as police would be called.

"Come on." She ushered her sister out of the car.

"You old bitch-made…" Storm made sure to slam the door and kick it, doing more damage to her foot than the car.

Skully grabbed her sister by the arm, "Storm!"

Skully was working on them another ride, as Storm and the man continued their back and forth.

"Hey!" She looked up to see Law leaning over his passenger seat. "I know how you feel about talking to strangers, would you take a ride from one?"

She turned to her sister and rolled her eyes to the ceiling. "You get in the front seat." She huffed. "I could just smack you right now."

Storm made herself comfortable removing her heels.

"Sup?" Storm looked over at Law, then back in the backseat at her sister. "Who is this Skully, because I know you don't got no friends that I don't know about."

"Storm turn around and put your seatbelt on."

"Girl." Storm rolled her eyes sitting back straight. She leaned in to turn up the radio a little.

They still had a way to go before they would be out of the mini-traffic jam.

"Well, thank you- whoever you are."

"What the hell?"

The sound of the relentless horn blowing behind them caught all their attention.

"Who the…"

The car sped around and in front of them forcing Law to stop the car to avoid a crash.

Storm reached over to blow the horn herself. Completely oblivious to what was really going on until the passenger door opened, and he put her over his shoulder to carry her to the car. "Brennon?" She questioned.

Once he had sat her in the passenger seat and fastened her into the seatbelt, he walked back toward the car.

Skully's eyes got big as she hopped out of the backseat.

"Bren-" She held up her hand.

"Skully?" Brennon hadn't even realized she was in the backseat. "What's going on? Your sister calls me talking shit, then I pull up…"

"It's a long story. He's my…" She looked back at Law who now stood leaning against his driver's door, arms crossed. "…Friend." She finished. "He was just being nice since your wife got us kicked out of our Uber."

"Oh…" Brennon instantly relaxed, he couldn't help but release a laugh. "My bad." He held up a hand to Law, who simply nodded his head. "Well, you come on sis."

"You won't mind taking me, home, would you?" Skully looked back once more.

Law shook his head.

"Aight. Text me. You better take her home man." He pointed past her to Law.

"Boy," Skully laughed. "I'm too grown. You get her home!" She started walking around to the passenger seat.

"Do you- do you want me to stop?" Brennon panted.

Please let the answer be no because he didn't know if he had that type of willpower.

"No-no." Storm gripped his back for leverage. "Just keep going."

Brennon closed his eyes, she felt good- too good to him. Better than that.

He opened his eyes and kissed her passionately. He was at the brink, but as he sped up his strokes, he could see her wince in pain.

His pleasure couldn't come at the expense of her pain.

He pulled out and rolled over beside her.

"I told you not to stop." Storm wined.

"Yeah well, your body told me something else. You're all tense." Brennon knew better. "You weren't enjoying it."

"Yes, I was." Storm lied.

"I know you Storm…"

Storm took a sharp breath. "I'm sorry baby. I think I just- I had a lot to drink."

"Oh, I know. You were all in my ear in the car on your cut-up shit."

"I'm sorry."

"Don't be." He shook his head. "Babe, you don't think you're pregnant, do you?"

Their sex was fire. He knew the ins and outs of her

body, which was why lately he knew something was off.

"No." Storm answered too quickly. Then he saw her considering it. "I mean I hope not, I was drinking like a fish tonight." She paused, shaking her head. "Nahh..."

They looked over at one another for a short while, "I mean... I was slanging that thang back when you could take it."

Storm hit him playfully in the arm, "Now you got jokes."

"I'm messing with you, babe." He kissed the side of her face. "I'll go get a test in the morning."

Just as he leaned in to give her a kiss on the lips, her mouth filled with saliva, as she gagged.

He reached over to retrieve the mini trash can under their bedside table. "Let you out the house one night..." He shook his head.

"Well, this is my humble abode," Skully commented when they arrived at her complex. "Thanks for the ride."

"Did I really have a choice?" He retorted.

"Yes, and you still chose to bring me home. Thank you." She repeated. She stalled for a minute before she continued. "Look, I realize I probably come off a type of way but..." She stopped herself before she could even say too much and reached for the door handle.

"Good night. Or good morning depending on how you look at it."

"Yep." He nodded.

She stepped out of the car but found herself turning back.

"Was there something else?" He rolled the window down.

"I'm just trying to figure out how you call yourself being interested in me and you don't even have the decency to ask for my number." She placed her arms in the window.

"I could play games right along with you, but I'd rather not. No need to try to force anything when your whole demeanor says you're closed off and you yourself said you're not interested."

"I'm not closed off. I'm whatever you bring out of me." She corrected him. "I wasn't interested and then I changed my mind." She shrugged. "So, what's it gon be?"

"Take my number. You'll either call or you won't. Balls in your cart."

"Hey babe." Storm entered the bathroom and hopped on the sink.

"Good morning." He leaned in to kiss her before refocusing his attention to the shape-up he was giving himself.

She started unpackaging the pregnancy, "Well. I'm going to take this test."

The three minutes that passed while they waited, they filled with small talk, until finally Storm could breathe a sigh of relief. "Well... I'm not pregnant!"

"Damn you happy as hell." He chuckled.

"No. I just think now we can plan it. Take away that element of surprise and figure out what we really want."

"I want whatever you want. Brennon nodded his head, "I'm ready only if you are. I know the pregnancy was tough for you..."

"Tough for us." Storm corrected.

"You're right, but you've got to know that I've grown as a man, husband, and father. I got you, and I got us."

"Then I guess we better make some room because this family's about to grow. We're having another baby!" Skully squealed.

He leaned over to give her a kiss on the forehead.

"What up Lee?" Skully walked into his office in the back of the shop the following day.

"You tell me." He wore a sneaky grin.

Skully's eyebrows furrowed in confusion. "Um... you know something I don't?"

"Nah, I'm just messing with you." He chuckled. "Sit down. Let's talk business."

"My type of talk." She nodded happily taking a seat.

"I wanted to talk to you about the Art Villain convention..."

"Don't play with me right now."

The Art Villain convention was any upcoming artist's dream. It was an invite-only convention. The sort of thing that could change your career if you let it, just on the connections you could make and hands you could shake alone.

"I think you're ready. I know you're ready." He corrected himself.

"Lee!" She exclaimed reaching across to give him a hug. "This is so dope. Like I still don't know what to say."

"Don't speak on it. Flight's book. Hotels covered."

" Well, I got to get ready for a client. Had me thinking I was in trouble."

"You could be." He grinned. "What you got going with Law?"

"I don't even know why that's a question. That's just a client to me."

"Aight then. Keep it that way."

———

"No-no-no." Nari shook her head. "Don't y'all start it."

"We're just having a simple conversation." Storm defended.

"No, that's how it always starts," Nari replied. "One-minute y'all talking about grits, the next y'all arguing about everything. Including shit that has absolutely nothing to do with grits!"

"I'm just saying… you sleep next to a nigga that puts sugar in grits, every night." Storm concluded. "Let that sink in." she pointed.

Nari shook her head. She had never seen two people who could argue about anything.

"Um… what you over there smiling about?" Storm's attention diverted to her sister.

"Huh?"

"If you can huh you can hear." Without hesitation, Storm snatched the phone from her sister's hand.

She had been tagged in a post from Law. The first slide was a picture of his sister, the next was of the tattoo.

In so many words, he was thanking her and expressing how much the dedication piece meant to him, as well as shouting her out for being a dope artist.

"Wow." Storm smiled. "You never cease to amaze me. This looks so good." She complimented her.

"Thank ya, thank ya. I'm impressed with myself." Skully boasted. "I did that."

"Let me see." Torrian came looking over their shoulder. "Hold up." Torrian snapped his finger. "Why do I feel like I know her?"

"Here you go, you always know some bitches, huh?" Nari rolled her eyes, suddenly interested in seeing the tattoo herself.

"Look at you. Always got some petty shit to say."

"Shut up." Nari was raking her mind, trying to figure exactly why she felt like she'd seen her somewhere else. "I don't even know... it might come back to me. Maybe if I didn't have people arguing about grits my mind wouldn't be so scrambled right now."

Just like that, the conversation was back light, but Skully's mind was still a little curious about what had happened with Law's sister.

"The least you could do is get the door!!" Skully yelled she banged on Ebony's bedroom door on her way to answer the front door. "Since you're up making all that damn noise!!"

Skully opened the door and cringed at the sight of their landlord Mr. Brown.

"How are you, Mr. Brown?" She forced a smile. It wasn't that she had to fake it with him. He was easily one of the nicest men she had ever met.

He let out a heavy sigh. "I'm sorry Skully. I hate to do this, but my hands are tied. This is the 3rd noise complaint this month. On top of things I've just been tolerating for months. I know it's not you, but of course you're a package deal. You're going to have to be out by the end of the month."

Mr. Brown went on to further explain the logistics.

"I assume you'll relay the message."

"I'll relay the message alright." She muttered.

All Skully could think of was the expediated move that she wasn't prepared for. She hadn't even found a place she liked yet.

"Thank you, Mr. Brown." Her bitterness wasn't directed toward him personally, but she was very much bitter.

3

"*I* just had an epiphany!" Kaice gasped dramatically. "What if my soulmate got swallowed or aborted? Wouldn't that make so much sense?"

"How unfortunate." Storm shook her head.

"Mama, what does aborted mean?" Jelani asked.

"See what you've done." Storm sighed. "Jelani go get your tablet."

"Uh-uh, is this pork?" Kaice turned up her nose.

"Yeah, and?" Storm retorted.

"You know my dietary restrictions. I can't just be eating anything."

"When did this hoe become so selective of what meat she puts in her mouth?" Skully butted in. "It was Devonte, Marcus, Jacoby, about 3 Shawn's…" She cracked. "That mouth can do a whole DMX challenge."

Kaice gave her the middle finger, as they all 3 cracked up.

"Sorry Kaice. No pescatarian-friendly meal tonight." Storm stated as they headed back into the dining room to join the others.

"So, Skully I got a friend who's tryna get tatted," Torrian spoke.

"Um, huh. Your last friend was trying to do more than get tatted." Skully replied. "Don't send no more of them wild lil niggas my way."

"Send em!" Storm blurted out. "Send em all her way. Skully, you need you a lil boo."

"I do not." Skully denied. "I'm living my life right now. Having fun right now."

"Fun?"

"Get off my sis's case." Brennon said.

"Please. I got enough on my plate. I now have to be out of my apartment at the end of the month." Skully rolled her eyes. "I mean if I had everything situated and could move today I would. That's not the case though, so essentially Ebony has screwed me once again."

Skully had sat on the news for a couple of days and she was still just as pressed.

"I knew there was a reason I never liked that girl. I haven't trusted an Ebony since Player's Club you know I'm always right." Storm shook her head. "Just let me come talk to her."

"No. We not about to make a bad situation worse."

"Well, you know there's always room for you here."

"We'll see." Skully sighed. "Just a minor lil setback. I've been kicked out of better places." Sometimes she just had to crack a joke to keep from feeling like a joke.

She loved her sister, but having to move back in with her would just be a reminder of how Storm seemingly had it all together, and once again she'd fallen short.

"We didn't want you moving in with us anyway." Storm teased, trying to lighten her sister's mood. "You'll figure it out." She winked. "You always do."

"Let me in!" Skully spoke into the system.

Moments later she heard the buzz, and the apartment doors opened. Skully scurried inside, there was a man not far behind and she could tell he intended for her to hold the door for him. It just didn't feel safe, it was after 11 pm.

Skully walked inside and headed toward the elevator, pressing 6 when she was inside.

Law: You tryna come over?

That had been the text she had received about an hour and a half earlier while still at her sister's.

Naturally, Skully had taken it the wrong way initially. Especially since he had had her number for over a week, and that was the first time he was using it at that time.

Law must've seen the error of his ways by her lack

of response because he quickly called and explained. He had been wanting to get up with her, however, his schedule had been so hectic he couldn't find the time. He really didn't even have it then, he'd been studying the day away but really wanted to see her.

There weren't very many men who could've convinced her, but for some reason she believed him.

It was usually a lot easier to be her usual anti-self, but with him, she felt compelled. He'd caught her interest, and now he had it.

"Hi." She smiled slyly when he opened the door.

He looked as relaxed as expected in a white t-shirt, and gray sweats. The sweats did it.

She too looked super chill, he took her in. From her black and red turban atop of her head, to the black, red, and white air max on her feet. Skully was petite, especially next to him. With a baby face, pierced nose, and right arm that was covered in colorful art down to her wrist. Then there was the tattoo, just at the edge of her hairline, that was hard to miss.

"Hey," He held the door open for her. Skully was already stepping out of her shoes. "You don't have to do that."

"Force of habit," Skully replied. She took a glance over the *very* nice apartment. It was very spacious and well-decorated.

"I like your place." She complimented.

"Thanks." He led the way to the dining room table

where he had all his things laid out from scattered sheets of paper, a couple of books, and a laptop.

"So, this is where all the magic happens." She joked taking a seat at the table furnished with some of the most comfortable chairs Skully had ever sat in.

She placed her bag on the edge of the chair and pulled out her own sketchbook and materials.

"I didn't want to just be watching you." She explained. "I didn't want to be bored."

"You don't think I can entertain you?" He smirked.

She looked up at him and away quickly.

"Can I get you anything to drink? Eat? Anything?"

"Just water."

He came around to the table with her water and some chips. They quickly fell into an easy routine of just doing their thing.

Skully walked around to the kitchen to wash her hands and was right in his bag of chips when she returned.

"Yeah okay. Ms. Just water." He teased.

"I can't turn down chips, come on now."

An hour later, she sat at the counter while they took a food break.

"How much longer you got to go?" Skully asked.

"This is the last stretch. Once I finish this semester I'm out." He answered.

"Congratulations! Good for you. I tried the college thing it didn't work."

"What was your major?"

"Business of course, the major of all the people who have no clue what they want to do with their lives."

He chuckled, "You just called it quits?"

"I actually got kicked out," she clarified. "Got caught doing tattoos in my dorms. There were so many problems with that, starting with me not being licensed to do so. I wasn't expelled infinitely but I knew when it happened, I wasn't going back."

"How'd your peoples feel about that?"

"My mama said she was surprised I even made it as long as I did." Skully laughed. "Luckily, she has the perfect daughter in Storm so when I screw up, she still has something to be proud of."

"I'm sure she's just as proud of you. That's just how parents are."

"I don't doubt that. Treasure she's- she's different. That's OG love her to death."

"What about your father?"

"Loved that man too. The old silent killer caught up to him, high blood pressure."

"Sorry to hear that." He cleared his throat.

"No worries, it happened my senior year in high school I've mourned. Besides, he was a happy man. He lived a fun life." She took another bite of her burger. "What about you? You all up in my business."

"Well… growing up it was always me, my sister, and my brother it was cool. My ma and pops divorced when we were 12. Ma has been remarried for 7 years now. She found a good dude." He nodded. "Haven't seen my pops in a committed relationship since. Got five more siblings though, I got an 8-month-old little brother." He chuckled shaking his head in disbelief.

"Papa was a-rollin' stone, huh?"

"I guess." He shrugged. "I'm just glad my mama found her somebody better."

Skully nodded her head, "I take it you don't get your relationship habits from him."

"Nah. I mean don't get me wrong, he's taught me plenty, but I think I could teach him a thing or 2 about how to love a woman. Truthfully, I think my mama's the one he let get away and he still hasn't gotten over that."

"Now that's a lesson for that ass." She pointed to him.

"Yeah, when you find that one don't just do the work to get her, put in that overtime to keep her."

"So, there's clearly no woman being kept by you."

"Nope, I'm as single as it gets. Not even looking really, I got too much on my plate." He spoke honestly. "That love shit is taxing."

"I completely agree." She nodded. "I couldn't have said it better myself."

"But that's the crazy thing… my mama told me the moment she stopped looking for love that's when it found her. Love is the type of shit that just takes over it doesn't really care what you want."

Skully took the final bite of her burger. "I hope someone finds my mother. She's a beautiful woman, and she deserves it. I just think she thinks it's some type of betrayal to daddy like he wouldn't want her to be happy."

"It's tough."

"It is." She let out a heavy sigh.

She got up to clear his mess and hers.

"I got you." When he reached, their hands touched, and she instantly felt a shudder up her spine.

Skully pulled back with a quickness. "No, I can do it." She insisted.

When she did return, she prepared herself to get ready to go. "Well, you've been a gracious host. It's getting late. I should head out."

"Yeah," he sighed. "I appreciate you coming. This was coo."

$\mathcal{O}$ver the next couple of weeks that passed, Skully and Law seemed to fall into the routine of her ending up coming over by the end of every night.

"Hi." She smiled shyly.

"Hey." Hey replied.

"You know these are booty call hours," Skully accused placed a hand on her hip. "So, what does that say about what you really think about me?" She stepped out of her shoes.

In that one step, Skully was already halfway to relaxation.

"What does you coming over say?" He shot back.

"Not what you think it says," Skully replied with an arched eyebrow. "So, don't even think you're finessing me out my panties."

"What?" Law couldn't do anything but laugh.

Skully shimmied out of her jeans-revealing the workout shorts underneath, removed her hoodie, and placed them both on the wooden dining room chair. Then pulled her hair into a bun.

"Comfortable, yet?" He teased.

"Not yet." She replied walking over to the comfortable couch and flopping down on it. "Oh wait…" she scanned the side table for the remote kicking her feet up once she found it. "Do you have a blanket?" She grinned.

He shook his head with a chuckle. He returned with a blanket in hand. "Anything else ma'am? Some popcorn? Water? A drink?"

"Now that you mention it… I am a little parched. A drink sounds lovely."

He licked his lips. "I got you, but you know the guest card is only valid for a couple more visits."

"I'll have worn out my welcome by then. By that point, you won't even want me around."

Law returned with a glass for himself and her. "I doubt that. Cheers. To two busy people trying to figure out if the other is worth making the time we don't have."

"Cheers." She smiled.

They downed the drinks, "This is me making time by the way."

"This is me appreciating you for it."

"By bossing me around?"

"By not being closed off." She corrected him.

"Another drink? Please." She added with a friendly smile.

―――――――

"That was a good call I'll admit," Law admitted. "I can't lie I didn't think the movie would even hold my attention."

"Told you," Skully smirked. "I rarely have the time to watch tv, but when I do best believe it's gon be something good. I live for good dialogue."

They had just finished the Netflix original, *Malcolm & Marie.* They didn't talk at all during the movie, which Skully appreciated because that was a pet peeve of hers.

"It was definitely a conversation starter."

"It was real. I mean you women gon keep up an argument just for the argument's sake." He commented.

"Oh yeah?" Her eyebrow hiked. "That's what you got out of that? Not that, the whole time all Marie wanted was a simple thank you and the entire argument could've been avoided but it would've just been too much like right for Malcolm to give her that."

"I could argue that's more of a woman play. They just couldn't make Malcolm no perfect nigga so that's the angle that took. Why even bring that up at such a prime time in his life? He was having his moment, and she couldn't have it. Why? Because women like to argue!"

"I'm not biting." She shook her head.

"I prefer not to argue at all, but when faced with an argument I know there's no way out. Arguing with a woman builds characters." He stated. "I learned a long time ago with my mother. You just got to take it on the chin. You'll never win. You're always wrong. Don't say too much, don't say too little because then you're not listening, and you can't let her know that even though you tuned out 30 minutes ago."

Skully chuckled as she answered her vibrating cell-phone. "Hello." She answered.

"Where are you?" Storm questioned.

"Uh, where are you?" Skully retorted.

"At your house! Ready to pack up your shit. I brought you a whole crew. Where are you?"

"I completely forgot. I'm on my way." She ended the call. She turned to Law. "Hate to cut the night short, but I do have to go. I was supposed to be meeting my sister so she can help me pack. Since I'm being put out." She said it jokingly but the whole situation truly annoyed the hell out of her.

"Need another hand?"

"I mean… if you're offering. I do have a lot of things." She shrugged.

Law was already standing to his feet. "I'll drive."

"Is that your ploy to get me back here?"

"Maybe."

"I'm going to warn you, I have an idiot for a roommate," Skully explained as she unlocked her door. "Who knows…"

Before she could even finish her sentence, she had already unlocked the door and could hear the commotion going on.

They'd walked in on an argument between Ebony and Storm.

The two already didn't care for each other, so her being the cause of Skully being put out was like fuel to fire. Storm wasn't the person to hold her tongue, so Skully could only imagine how whatever this was had gotten started.

"You a nothing ass, leashing ass bitch and I've been telling my sister…"

"Storm!" Skully began pushing her sister down the hall until they were in the room.

She could hear Kaice and Ebony exchange a few words before the front door slammed shut.

"Sorry." She addressed Law.

"Oh, hey Law!" Storm greeted him with a smile. "We gotta stop meeting like this. You catching me snapping on people. You here to help us pack?" She placed a hand on her hip.

"That's the plan. Don't seem like much packing was going on."

"Sorry you had to see me like that, I'm really not that person. Some people just bring it out of you."

Storm apologized. "Something wrong with all of them hoes named Ebony."

They could all laugh at that as they started the process of starting the packing process.

"Your room is dope." He complimented looking around.

Skully was one of those people who had so much stuff it was hard to know what to do with it all, still everything had a place and had to be put away properly.

Her room was like a mini art gallery, a combination of her own work as well as others whose work she enjoyed. Including a portrait Lee had done of her that she loved.

"Thank you," Skully replied.

"You did these two, didn't you?" He pointed.

"Those are your favorites, huh?" She smirked, before nodding her head in confirmation. "Yeah, those are mine."

Over the hour and a half that they busied themselves packing away, they talked and laughed over various different topics.

"I can't believe ma is not coming home for Thanksgiving." Storm changed the subject. "Just don't even feel right. Who's supposed to cook the macaroni?"

"I can bring it as my dish this year," Skully suggested.

"Okay, so no macaroni this year." Storm concluded. "Got it."

"Forget you. She has a life too, maybe even a man."

"You think?" Storm wondered.

"I hope. We've seen mama carry around this guilt like moving on means she loved daddy any less. We all love daddy, and I know he would want to see her happy again. It's okay to find love again."

"If that's the case, she should've just brought him too. I wouldn't care. I miss my old lady."

"She's probably scared you'd scare him off. I would be."

Storm gave her the middle finger.

"You should join us for Thanksgiving," Kaice stated, pointing to Law.

"Kaice!"

"What?!?"

"He has his own family that I'm sure he would love to spend Thanksgiving with."

"Everybody don't like their family, okay? Why do you think I'm always with y'all?" Kaice replied.

"Since she put it out there, the invitation is definitely open." Storm confirmed. "All I ask is that you bring a dish of your choice. Just let it be something you're good at cooking. Not like this one and her macaroni."

"It can't be that bad." Law defended.

"Don't be so sure. If you'd tried it, you'd be knocking it too." Storm assured him.

"Dually noted. I'll keep that in mind. That invite

too." He glanced over at Skully who still looked to be uncomfortable.

"Alright, let's wrap this up. I think we've done enough for the night."

"Aw, how you gon put us out? That's why you getting put out now!" Storm joked. "Too soon?" She turned to see her sister's frowning face.

"Too soon," Skully confirmed straight-faced.

"Well, we're out then." Storm replied standing to her feet. "You're welcome by the way."

"Thank you."

"It was nice meeting you." Kaice waved to Law.

"Bye Law." Storm waved. "Don't be getting too comfortable with my sister." She warned.

"Sorry about that, my sister can unintentionally be a lot sometimes. Forget about that Thanksgiving invite too."

"Damn, so I don't even get to try that macaroni."

"Well, I mean…"

Law chuckled, "It's all good. I appreciate the invite anyway." He let out a heavy sigh. "The holidays are kind of hard for us. I know that it's something you never get over, it just still feels too fresh."

"I'm so sorry." She reached out to grab his hand. It was like instinct. "I know it's a lot, but you know at least your family has each other to get through it. Having my sister and mama has always been the best thing I've had going for me."

"Yeah."

Skully nodded her head. "I'm here. If you need me."

The words came out before she even realized the weight of them. She didn't even know this man like that, this certainly didn't help with the guard she was trying to keep up.

What would she do if he actually did need her?

"I appreciate that."

———

"I just want to know who y'all think y'all is." Wilma placed her hand on her hip with a grunt. "Got my son acting all saditty. Like he too good to get married in the church he grew up in."

They were in the car, on the way to some dress shops and Wilma's mouth hadn't stopped moving since they left the house.

Camile learned a long time ago Wilma was the type of woman that was going to make her own scenarios in her head and call it reality.

For as long as she had dreamed of having a wedding, it had been somewhere on a beach in the sun and that was exactly what she was getting.

"What's good for the goose is good for the gander." Wilma continued. "Same church I got married in."

"All 3 times?" Storm quipped.

Camile wasn't going to say it, but she was glad Storm was around to do so.

It wasn't that Camile didn't like her mother-in-law.

She was just one of those older women that thought her age warranted respect, whether she gave others that same respect or not. That's just not how life worked.

"Uh uh. Don't come for me Storm." Wilma shook her head. "I don't understand why y'all got to be policing me like I can't pick out my own dress."

"Because you can't." Camile cackled. "That dress was a mess and I'm not letting you go out sad ma dukes."

"No ma'am, no ma'am." Wilma protest. "I got that straight out of the catalog."

"And that's the problem." Storm pointed. "Let's try something else."

"Now listen here, I'm not wearing none of that Forever 21 mess, I'm far removed from my twenties-honey child. And none of that Fashion Nova, I'll leave that to the young hussies and harlots."

"Oy vey, this is going to be a long day." Camile massaged her temples.

"Well gals, I've got to get out of here." Kaice returned after being M.I.A. for a good 40 minutes with completely different clothes on and a bag in hand.

"I know you fucking lying." Storm gawked. "Where are you going?"

"To hell if I don't pray." Kaice quipped.

"I thought you didn't want to be a playa no more."
Skully shook her head. "What happen Big Pun?"

Kaice gave her the middle finger. "Some days I
think I'm ready to get out these streets and others... I
realize, *I just might be a hoe.*" She sung.

"Do you boo." Camile held up her glass to her. "Be
safe. Text us when you get to where you're going and
when you leave. Well... if you leave."

"Later!"

"Got to love her."

"Do you?" Skully challenged.

"I mean, with Kaice she's just going to do her, and I
respect it. I mean she's single." Nari shrugged. "And
don't they say all women should go through a hoe
phase in their life. Well, not saying Kaice's a hoe or
anything." She clarified.

"Well, she is." Storm teased. "I wouldn't know girl.
I've been with Brennon since I was 16 and I'm just fine.
Not missing nothing out here in these streets."

"Only way you could know this, is if you were out
here in them." Camile rolled her head to Storm
wearing a sneaky grin.

"What's tea?" Skully looked between the two.

"What?" Storm's face wore guilt all over it.

"Okay, somebody get to talking!" Skully demanded
as Camile took another swig of her wine.

"Okay, okay." Storm let out a heavy sigh. "A long-
long-long-long..."

"Stop stalling!"

"A long time ago. You know when everyone up and left me for college…."

Originally, Skully was supposed to go to U of L as well, but on a whim had decided to go off on adventures of her own.

Truth be told, she had known a while before she broke the news to Storm. She just had a hard time telling her.

While Brennon was always going away because of better scholarship opportunities out of state.

"And you know me, and Brennon had that patch where the long-distance was too much for us, and we broke up." Storm recounted the story. "I was at home, refund checks out the ass, and ma wasn't expecting much out of me other than good grades, and I did that…"

"We know, we know." Skully rolled her eyes. "You got the degree, I didn't. Can we get to the tea?"

"You know how me and Lee were basically doing everything together?"

"Yeah, and?"

"Well, we literally did *everything* together."

Skully gasped, covering her mouth in shock. Never in a million years would she have thought as close as Lee and Storm had been that they'd crossed those lines.

"Does Brennon know?"

"Of course. We don't keep secrets. Mainly, because I can't lie for shit and, also because what could he really do? I was single." Storm stated. "Plus, he wasn't being no saint so… anyway. Lee and I came to our senses and realized we were just friends."

"Yeah, yeah. All that realization shit is alright, but the thing is this… you and Lee are still friends currently. How does that fly?"

"For starters I'm grown. Secondly, Brennon is not an insecure man."

"Well call me muthafuckin Issa Rae because I don't want my man being friends with someone he's been involved with. Like ever. I want you to forget she exists."

"No lie, Jeremiah would have a conniption." Camile shook her head. "And it's not an insecurity thing, it's just… I personally make that decision myself out of respect."

"I forget y'all weird anyway. I mean Kaice's always going out with the boys, kicking it with Brennon. I get that they're friends, but the places my head would go. I'd have to be admitted."

Well, hell he doesn't even like any of my friends but y'all." She added with a chuckle.

"Yeah, but Kaice is family. I mean her and Brennon were always really good friends aside from our rela-tionship." Storm defended.

"Yeah, like you and Lee." Nari quipped.

"Alright, we've had enough tea." Camile was prepared to change the subject.

"Nah, let's spill tea." Storm insisted. "Let's get into some chami-mile tea."

"Girl what?"

"I was trying to make a play on chamomile tea. Either way since we're spilling other people's tea, I got you Camile. You know I got tea."

The next couple of days were extremely busy for Skully. She had a bunch of appointments and had gone on 3 different apartment tours.

Finding a decent-priced, nice apartment that was also in a good part of the city within good proximity to work was proving to be harder than she thought.

"Knock, knock." The shop's receptionist Tweety appeared at her door. "There someone here to see you girl."

She looked at the time and then up at him, "Who?"

She didn't have any more clients for the day.

That had been intentional, she had just finished up a 6-hour session, that had started at 6 am to work around her client's schedule. It was well worth it, but she was good and tired.

"Chile, I don't know," Tweety smirked. "I'm just mad he's not here to see me."

She had a gut feeling about who it was, which put a little pep in her step when she went to see.

"Hi." She greeted him.

No matter how many times she saw him, it was like the initial shock of an athlete hopping in an ice bath.

She had to brace herself not to jump all over him.

God had taken his time, then doubled back to take a little more just in case he forgot something.

"How are you?" He asked.

He surprised her with the hug that she didn't even know she needed.

"Good." She cleared her throat, stepping back to fully take him in.

Even in his simplicity, he looked so damn good. In a pair of black jeans, a black and blue plaid shirt with a blue jean jacket over it, a pair of blue and black Air Jordan 1's and a black beanie.

"This is a surprise."

"I know. Daytime, right?" He smirked.

She smiled. "Right. So, what's up?"

"Well, I know you're a busy woman, but I was hoping I caught you at a good time. Enough time to get lunch?"

"Actually, you couldn't have caught me at a better time. I was actually just packing up..."

He was already walking up to her, insisting to help her. "Let me help you out."

"No, it's okay. You can just wait out here."

"Nah." Was his simple response. "Just tell me what to do. I know that's no problem for you."

She laughed, hitting him playfully on the arm.

"You two kids be safe." Tweety grinned. "Have fun. Do everything I would." He took another look at Law. "And then some." He cackled.

"Don't do too much Tweety." She shook her head.

"I wouldn't be me if I didn't," Tweety replied with a chuckle. "I'll need deets later."

"Stay out my business Tweety."

"Honey, I'm just glad you got some."

Law held the door open for her.

"Whoa, whoa…" Just as they were heading out, Lee was coming in. "What do we have here?"

"What's up, Cuz?" Law greeted him.

"Not a whole lot." Lee looked from him to Skully. "Skully- Skull."

"Hi Lee." She smiled. "I'm going to take my stuff to the car. I'll follow behind you."

"I'll drive. I can bring you back to your car."

Skully had a little reluctance, "Okay." She waved to Lee. "Later, Lee." She walked over to her car.

"You still moving forward on that, Fam?" Lee questioned. "Even though you and Tatum wishy, washy as a laundry mat?"

"That's over with."

Lee let out a heavy sigh. "As you said, I got too much of my own business to be in anybody else's. Skully's like a little sister though, hard as her exterior might be, she's a good girl at heart and she's been through a hell of a lot. Don't put her through anymore."

Skully returned by Law's side, "You ready?"

"I can't even believe that." Law shook his head. "So, someone actually got R. Kelly King of R&B tattooed on their arm?"

Day had turned to night, and they still weren't tired of each other.

They ended up back at his place being that hers was covered in boxes.

Skully nodded her head. "You have to give the people what they want, but I just can't believe someone would actually want that."

Law chuckled. "Yeah, that's crazy. I bet you got a bunch of wild stories."

"Too many." She confirmed. "It's not all crazy though. I love the meaningful tattoos, with sentiment. Like yours."

Conversation between them flowed naturally.

"Yeah, I think I found my new favorite tattoo artist. I might have to have you do my next one too."

She smiled. "After that first tattoo, I think we all become ink junkies. All of mine mean something to me though."

"What's the meaning of this one?"

"What?" Skully's eyebrows furrowed in confusion. "This." He stroked her cheek with his hand and took his thumb along her hairline and back down to her ear. Where in cursive letters she had the words *'Never Trust'* inked.

"What about it?" She wondered.

"Just why? You have such a beautiful face."

Skully's tattoos were cause for conversation more times than not. However, she was no stranger to compliments on her beauty.

She had brown almond-shaped eyes, naturally long lashes, and full eyebrows.

Her big, rounded nose, along with her full juicy lips, and the beauty mark just above them, that used to make her a target for teasing before she grew into her beautiful features.

"Wow... I see your tattoos as art and that's how you view mine? Have I ruined my beautiful face?"

"Maybe that didn't come outright. You're a gorgeous woman. I don't think there's much that could change that. Unless your insides didn't match."

"Wouldn't you like to know what it's like inside me." she grinned.

He chuckled, shaking his head. "So, you don't trust anyone?" He was looking her right in the eyes. "You don't think you could ever trust me?" He added.

"Do you think you could earn my trust?" She challenged.

"All I can do is try."

"You have to try, really, really hard." She reiterated. "Thank you for having me over. Even though it's still hella sus, never seen you in the daytime. I don't know about you." She pointed with a smirk.

He used his thumb to tuck her hair securely behind her ear.

He knew what he wanted to do, so he went for it and she turned her head to the side to dodge it.

"Let's get back to these movies." She insisted grabbing the remote.

On the inside she was cussing herself out.

It wasn't like she didn't want to kiss him or mind him kissing her.

It just seemed like a step in the direction that scared the hell out of Skully.

———

"Don't work at MAC but I'll beat a bitch face," Nari rapped along as she showed off her beat in her Instagram video. "I just beat my face." She stuck out her tongue as Torrian walked up behind her in the mirror. He wrapped an arm securely around her neck and kissed her.

She ended the video and posted it.

"You like my makeup babe?" Nari asked.

"Yeah, but you don't need it." He replied.

It was the sort of back-handed compliment that annoyed Nari. Why not just say her makeup looked good and leave it at that, whether he thought she needed it or not.

"Where you going anyway?" He questioned.

"Out for drinks." She answered. "With my girls."

"Storm and them?"

"No." She could see the change in his demeanor. "Let me guess, you have an attitude now? You gon try to tell me I can't go?"

"You gon do you regardless."

"Yep, you got an attitude, because you don't like my friend."

"They don't like me, and I don't like the bad influence they have on you."

"Bad influence?" Nari frowned. "Who are you, my father? Trying to dictate who my friends are and telling me what kind of influence they have on me as if I'm some monkey see, monkey do ass bitch."

"That's not what I'm saying. What I'm saying is they been hating on our relationship from jump. And then you got to do your make-up and do the most when you go out with them and you can't tell me they not out here telling you to be in the next niggas face."

Nari rolled her eyes. "What are you even talking about dude? You blowing me right now. I don't ever do this! I let you go out with your brother, don't ask any questions, and don't give you a hard time! I never go out of my way to kill your vibe like this!"

"You're right I'm killing your vibe. Ima let you go hoe in peace."

"You out your damn mind. You throwing around some wild allegations right now. Insinuating that I'm going out with my friends to cheat. You know the accuser is usually the guilty one."

"Go head on with that. We having a simple ass conversation, but since you're so pressed to go out with your hoe ass friends go do that!"

"And I will." She turned back to the mirror and finished off her look by doing her edges. "Sure will!" She turned her music up as far as it would go.

That wasn't the end of the argument.

Torrian was a get the last word type of person. You either danced to the beat of his drum or there was no drum.

When he returned to the bathroom, glaring at her through the mirror, she completely ignored him. Or tried her hardest to.

The closer he got to her, she could feel his breath on her neck.

"If you going, you changing." He stated it like it was law.

That was his idea of a compromise. When in actuality it was more like an ultimatum.

"No."

Nari saw nothing wrong with what she had on.

She wore a black corset crop top with mesh underwiring, a pair of ruched mesh leggings that hugged her figure, and her opened-toed, black shoes, with a chunky clear heel.

Her hair was pulled up in a top knot and her edges were laid. Not to mention she'd gotten back in her makeup bag and gave herself a full beat.

Torrian was just finding something to pick with.

"Take that shit off." He demanded.

Nari was somewhere in between being turned on and being pissed off.

"Make me." She challenged.

He turned her around and sat her up on the sink, before effortlessly unhooking the corset leaving her nude from the waist up. He was already reaching for her pants as he trailed kisses across her chest.

"Baby." She panted. "I have to call the girls and tell them I'm not coming."

It was over with. She was in for the night.

"You don't got to tell them shit." He slid her panties to the side and as he sunk slowly inside of her, continuing that same steady motion as she draped her arms around his neck.

He picked up the pace as her witness coated him and her moans played like music to his ears.

He pulled out, teasing her with the tip. Working his thumb in circular motions around her clit. "Damn my bad, don't you got somewhere to go?" He looked down at her cockily.

"Boy... stop playing with me."

5

"Now I know good and well you didn't roll up in here with this macaroni and cheese." Storm fussed. "Nobody asked for this dawg."

Skully laughed. "Forget you. This macaroni gon be gone in 2.5."

"No, it won't." Torrian shook his head. He lifted the aluminum foil to look at it. "I promise you it won't."

Skully hit him playfully on the arm.

"Auntie Skully, is that kraft's?" Jelani asked innocently. "We don't eat kraft's mac and cheese."

"Jelani!" Skully gawked.

"My baby knows the real when she sees it. This ain't it. Here Bren sit this over there with the undesirables. Rights next to Kaice's peach cobbler."

"I heard that!" Kaice called from the dining room.

"I meant you to!"

Thanksgiving for them was a mixture of friends and family.

"I also brought my broccoli casserole, but I guess y'all don't want that either."

"Who said that?" Brennon's interest was perked.

"We're here for the casserole now." Storm shook her head. "We love when you don't go chasing waterfalls and just stick to the rivers and the lakes that you're used to."

"Alright, everyone come on so we can bless this food!" Brennon announced. Brennon led them in prayer, and then everyone was ready to dig in.

Law had admittedly been in his feelings all day.

His day had started with him, his brother, and mother going to Amira's gravesite.

After that, he'd needed some time for himself.

Then he'd gone home to finish an assignment, he'd wait until the last minute to turn in.

Once he was dressed for the day, he went to kick it at his father's for a while, spending a little time with his younger siblings.

By the time he made it to his mother's house, it was much later and, as expected there was a full house. A combination of their family and Larry's.

There was plenty of food and drinks, kids running around, and adult conversation and games going on.

"Your pops cook today?" Lee questioned.

"Yeah, I was over there earlier. I'm sure everything's done by now." Law answered.

His mother was good too, but everyone knew Jeffery could cook his ass off.

"How's he holding up?" Lee asked. "It's been a lil minute since I've seen Jeffery."

"As good as any of us I guess," Law answered. "You know…"

"I know." Lee placed a hand on his cousin's shoulder. "Shit still fucks with me too."

A moment of silence passed between them. Neither men were the best at expressing their emotions.

"I might slide to Jeffery's though. You know I make all my rounds." Lee changed the subject.

"Yeah, I got some rounds to make myself."

"Well, you might want to start making them." Torrian entered the house. "I saw Tatum pulling up the same time I was."

"Ma." Law kissed his teeth. He walked over to her knowing she would be the only one to extend the invite because he sure didn't.

"What do you want me to say son? The girl practically invited herself." Kimba replied. "Say the word, and I'll stop inviting her to things, but you've never said she wasn't welcome."

"Invite who you want ma, but that's definitely my cue. Ima head out." He excused himself.

"Where are you-…"

"Out the back." He clarified. He didn't even want to risk running into Tatum.

The distance they'd put between themselves had been the best thing that could've happened.

Now that he was dealing with Skully he had more reason to steer clear of her.

"*THE COLOR PURPLE*!!!" Storm yelled.

Everyone cracked up laughing.

They were in the middle of what had turned into a heated game of Culture Tags.

"Give me another clue!" Brennon shouted. "That's all you keep saying!"

"Get me a new partner!" Storm demanded.

"You can't get a new partner." Camile was dying laughing. Everyone was. "That's your life partner boo you're stuck."

"You're wasting time Storm!" Brennon stressed. "Just skip it or give me another clue."

"It's one of the most known lines in *The Color Purple*!" Storm released an exasperated sigh.

"A different variation of the same damn clue." Brennon kissed his teeth. "Thanks a lot for that."

"YISYIKYII. Think about it. *The Color Purple*! Just think!"

"Time!" Skully shouted still laughing hysterically.

Storm slammed the cards back into the stack.

"Chill, chill, chill. Hand that stack over." Camile held her hand out. "We stealing those points."

Storm rolled her eyes handing it over.

"You should've given me another clue," Brennon argued.

"I don't know what to tell you, I gave you the best clue that there is. That should've been all you needed to know."

"Man, what was on the card?" Jeremiah questioned. "We'll just take those points off the table because I really got to know." He flipped the card over. "YISYISYII. You is smart, you is kind, you is important."

"Wowww!!!" Brennon exclaimed.

"You sat over here damn near having a conniption and you were giving this man the wrong clue. Ha!" Skully was laughing even harder at her sister's expense.

"Is that not the color purple?"

"NO!!!" they all shouted.

"Look at you, just loud and wrong." Kaice cracked. "That's from *The Help,* friend."

"Oh…" Storm's entire demeanor changed. "Well hell, y'all know I've never seen *The Color Purple.*"

"You've never seen *The Color Purple.*" Nari gasped.

"No, I haven't."

"But you've seen *The Help,* and you still led me in the wrong direction like that."

Now Storm was laughing at herself. "Sorry babe. I swear I thought that…."

"How do you think anything about a movie you've never even seen though?" Nari questioned.

"Whether you've seen it or not everyone knows those stand-out lines. Y'all know what the hell I'm talking about."

"No. We don't."

"You told Harpo to beat me!" Storm began calling out lines. "All my life I had to fight!"

"And apparently... you is smart, you is kind, you is important."

That would be a laugh for the rest of the night.

───────

"You came?" Skully offered a quick smile. She couldn't let on just how happy she was to see him, as if it had been forever instead of like two days.

They had been texting throughout the day, despite the circumstances Law had seemed to be in good spirits. Skully wasn't certain they'd be seeing each other though.

"I like to make my rounds," Law replied. "Figured I at least have room for pie before I call it a night."

"Come in." She led him through the dining room where Law greeted everyone.

"You can help yourself to whatever in the kitchen. Skully sit your ass down." Storm directed. "You not escaping this ass whooping."

"Did I mention I hate Dominoes?" Skully rolled her eyes.

"This cobbler it's off to the side, is it for someone specific? Can I have a piece?" Law called from the kitchen.

"NO!!!" Jelani blurted out abruptly. "Don't eat that cobbler!"

Everyone cracked up laughing. Having been the only one brave enough to try it, Jelani knew what they all didn't.

Storm knew from experience, her friend belonged a lot of places, but the kitchen wasn't one of them. She hadn't needed to taste it to no better. "Aw," Storm said. "My poor babies' taste buds are scarred."

"I don't know what you laughing for," Kaice addressed Skully. "Nobody's eating your macaroni either."

"I think it's pretty good." Law stood in the doorway with the plate.

"Aw isn't that cute," Kaice smirked. "He's trying to impress you."

"Your stomach is going to hate you later, brotha." Brennon shook his head.

———

"As you can see, I'm home." Skully announced, per request she'd facetimed him to let him know she'd

73

made it home safely. "It's actually quiet for once, surprise, surprise." She turned the key in the lock.

By the time she stepped inside, she was already stepping out of her shoes.

The apartment was eerily quiet. Unusually clean, she noticed that too. It wasn't that it was usually dirty, but it more so looked empty.

She reasoned Ebony had started moving out, *It's about time.*

She headed toward her bedroom.

"What are you about to get into?" He asked.

"The shower. The bed." Skully answered. "I have a busy, busy…" Skully stopped in her tracks, her phone dropped to the floor beside her but that didn't matter.

"Skully?!? Skully!!!"

"The door was open." Law made his presence known. He'd been standing at the doorway a few minutes but didn't speak until now.

Law hadn't been sure what he'd be walking into, but the sight of Skully sitting on the floor, back against the wall, made him feel a way.

He walked over to sit beside her.

Skully's eyes rolled to the ceiling, avoiding tears.

"Even when I think I'm getting my shit together… I still can't get right." Skully spoke. "Even when I try to do right by people, they do me wrong. So, what the fuck is the point?" She stressed. There came the tears. "What's the point?!?"

He reached his hand around her.

"I'm okay, I'm good." She pulled away and stood up. "If you can't tell, my roommate moved out and took not only her stuff but mine. Including thousands of dollars worth of tattoo equipment and some money, I was saving. A lot of money to me." She emphasized. She shook her head with a sigh. "I just can't believe this!"

"Look, I know that me being sorry doesn't change anything about your situation," Law began. "Let me know if I can do anything."

"No one uses that statement, like someone who can't even begin to be there for you the way you really need. Why'd you even come over here? I'm way more emotional than I care for you to see!" Skully replied. "I have a sudden need for money that I would never ask you for, and a place to stay that..." She let out a heavy sigh. "I'm sorry. I'm snapping on the wrong person right now."

"You're good. I get it."

"You couldn't possibly. I was wondering why I can't seem to catch a break with any of these apartments I've been looking at, turns out it does count as an eviction on my background. So yeah, when something can go bad for me it just does and I'm so fucking tired of it."

"Look, you're probably used to people saying it and not meaning it, but that's not me. I don't say things just to say them. So, if you need a place to stay, I have a guest room and no guest."

"Wh-what?" She stammered, looking over at him.

He had just blown her away.

If he hadn't heard them come out of his own mouth, he wouldn't have believed he was the source, either.

"If you need a place to stay, I got you. Matter of fact, you do need a place to stay." He was learning how she worked. She wasn't going to ask. Or admit that she needed anyone.

"So, you have a place to stay," Law stated.

"What is your motive? You don't even know me like that. Damn sure don't owe me anything… is that it? Am I going to owe you?"

"No. Not at all."

"Then what?"

"I'm just trying to be a friend to you."

"Is that all?"

"That's all. I know trust isn't your strong suit, but you're going to have to. I can't be worse than your last roommate."

Skully was able to at least crack a smile at that. "Can we just get out of here? I'll come get whatever's left of my stuff at some point but right now…" she let out an exasperated sigh. "I just can't…"

"Yeah, of course."

6

"**Ma**, what are you doing here?" Skully questioned.

It was 9 am on a Monday morning, and suddenly the entire day had just got interesting.

"She made me give her the address." Storm answered with a shrug. "I tried to warn you, but you didn't answer."

"Oh, so now I'm not welcomed to my own daughter's house?" Treasure placed a hand on her hip.

"It's not that." Skully shook her head. "You just can't be showing up to this man's house like this."

"Is this not where you lay your head?"

"Yes, I've been staying here."

"Then this is just as much your place as it is his. You got to run your guest list by him or something? Don't tell me you got another one of those Ike Turner type. Cause I got something for that this go-round." The

proof was in the purse, Treasure revealed the .22 inside.

"Ma!" Skully gasped.

"Chile, move out of my way." Treasure rushed her way in, and Storm wasn't far behind.

"I called." Storm replied passing her.

———————

"Wasn't sure if you'd be hungry, but I was sure you'd grill me if I came in here without enough food for you..." Law explained the whole way down the hall until he stopped at her food.

"I sure hope you brought enough food for everybody." Treasure replied. "What we eating?" She stood up and headed down the hall.

"Hey Law." Storm followed behind.

"My mother." She told him. "Treasure." She added. "I had no clue about this."

They went into the dining room to find Treasure and Storm had already begun making plates.

"Chinese." Treasure smiled. "My favorite. I'm Treasure by the way." She extended her hand.

"Law." He responded accepting with a pleasant smile.

"Sit down my girl," she instructed. "Sit down baby."

"I'm sure Law would like something to himself. We're already taking his food." Skully said.

"No, I'm good." Law denied.

"See, he's fine. You relax. I need to know all about any man my daughter is going to be living with."

"That's reasonable." Law nodded.

Treasure didn't meet any strangers. Within an hour and a half, she had pulled more out of Law, than Skully herself knew about him.

"I got to say, I'm a lot more comfortable with my daughters living conditions now." Treasure stated. "When I heard about everything that was going on, I knew I had to get down here for my babies. I was on the first thing smoking."

Three years prior Treasure was in a completely different space. She was still mourning the loss of her husband; she was treating depression with therapy and trying to pull herself out of a dark place.

The conclusion had been that she needed a fresh start. The girls had seen a great change in their mother since she moved to Florida.

When she did come home for holidays, or various occasions throughout the year it was always refreshing.

"My baby is resilient and I don't expect anything short of a major come back."

"Thanks ma." Skully smiled.

"Same thing I said," Storm replied. "Like Lady Michelle said, when they go low, we go high. Pay that girl no never mind."

"Is that what you had said?" Skully smirked as she excused herself for the bathroom.

"Law, what's your real angle here?" Treasure asked.

"Are you interested in a relationship with my daughter? Are there ulterior motives here? Does your kindness come at a cost?"

"I don't really get what you mean."

"You seem like an upstanding man and I can only hope it's authentic, but forgive me- I have to protect my daughter."

"That's understood. I just want to make it clear that I don't have any ulterior motives. The more I get to know Skully, the more I just want to be around her, because she's just genuinely a dope person. I saw an opportunity to help her, and I acted on it."

Treasure smiled. "I appreciate that. I really do and who knows…" She took a sip of her drink. "I mean, you're two young, attractive adults. My daughter really is a catch. If there's something more there, it wouldn't be wrong to explore it…"

"Okay!" Skully re-entered the room, displeased with the ladder of the conversation she'd walked in on. "Let's wrap this up."

"Bren you can't be serious right now." Storm pushed him off. "My mama is downstairs."

"Yes and not the least bit worried about what we're up here doing," Brennon replied. "Don't act like we didn't use to have sex all up in your people's house."

Storm shook her head. "Leave me alone. I really

have to finish this."

"Probably not even over there doing no real work. Over there hitting them keys hard as hell, for no reason."

Storm laughed, "You big mad, big baby. Take a cold shower." She hit him playfully with a pillow.

"I can't sleep."

"Cry baby, cry baby. Suck ya mama's titty."

"That's what I'm trying to do."

"You so stupid." She laughed. "I'm on my period anyway."

"I'm bout to go hop in the shower." He gave up, getting up to retrieve his boxer briefs from his drawer. "If you want to join me."

"I'll think about it."

He walked into the bathroom and began running the water. When he returned, he only had a towel wrapped around his waist, *"Throat babies," he sang. "I'm tryna give em' to you."*

"Brennon, go to hell." She burst out laughing.

"Come in."

Skully opened his bedroom door and stepped inside looking around his room.

This was her first time seeing what his bedroom looked like.

The black, red, and gray color scheme around the

room made sense with the togetherness that the rest of the house exuded. Law was simply a well-kept man.

"I just wanted to apologize. My mother's a lot, but she means no harm." Skully said. "Had I known she was even in town I would've given you a heads up."

"Not necessary." He shook his head. "You're just as welcomed to having people over as me. You don't need my permission."

Skully nodded her head.

He was in his bed still doing work. It was crunch time.

"I'll leave you to it then."

"Come back." He encouraged.

She entered the room the rest of the way, closing the door behind her.

"I didn't mean to interrupt. I shouldn't distract you from your work."

"You really should."

Skully lay across the end of his bed.

"This fucking case." He ran his hand over his head. "Mr. Dixon always said it'll drive you to drink if you let it. And I know part of the job is leaving the emotions at home, but I just get sick to my stomach when it comes to women and children."

"I can only imagine, literally, because I wear my heart on my sleeves too much for that. I'd turn into a vigilante out here in these streets."

"Who knew?"

"You don't think I can handle mine?"

"That I don't doubt. I didn't know you wore your heart on your sleeves."

"I have sensitivities to certain things."

"I'd like to see that."

"Maybe you will."

———

"So, you were all, I'm in a bind, Nate." Storm mimicked the words of Jada Pinkett from *Set it off.*

"You know what, that might be funny if I weren't really in a bind!" Skully hissed.

"About that, I'm a little offended." Storm retorted. "My doors are always open. There's always plenty of room here for you. You're telling me you'd rather live with a stranger than your family?"

"That's not even the case. I just don't want to intrude. You have Jelani and you're trying for another baby…"

"Girl, you know you could stay with us and it wouldn't be a problem."

"Skully, if you just wanted to move in with that fine ass chocolate man you should've just said that," Kaice commented. "I definitely wouldn't blame you. Don't nobody want to live with Storm."

"It's not like that."

"Not yet. Trust me. Right now, it's just a place to crash at and a shoulder to cry on. Before you know it, it'll be a bed to sleep in and a hard peen to hop on."

"You tried." Skully denied. "We're friends at best. I'm not sleeping with that man for a place to stay. That's more your speed than mine."

Kaice gave her the middle finger. "I mean we all know you hard-pressed for some hard peen. Now it's in-house. Even better!" Kaice quipped.

"Not gon happen."

"Girl, you are going to eat those words. Watch." Kaice said.

"She gon eat something else too." Storm quipped.

Kaice and Storm slapped hands as they laughed.

"Look, it's been like 3 years and even if it was 3 more- my..."

"3 years?!?" Leave it to Kaice to be as dramatic as possible.

"Yes, and what about it? What's wrong with being happily single & celibate."

"Chile, you know that don't even sound right together." Kaice shook her head. "Who the hell is happy and celibate?!?"

"I said the same thing." Storm threw her hands up. "Don't make no sense!"

"Kinda like horny and married Miss. Ma'am." Skully stated. "Why you not hoping on your husband's hard peen?"

Storm gasped dramatically. "Nothing is sacred anymore! I'm not telling you heffas anything else."

"Trouble in paradise?" Kaice asked.

"No." Storm denied.

Kaice and Skully both looked over at her, unconvinced.

"It's just... I don't know what's going on with me." Storm confessed. "I'm moody, my weight is fluctuating, and hella emotional for no reason. Yet, I'm not pregnant. Make it make sense."

"Uh, did somebody say menopause?" Kaice joked.

"The thing is, I didn't know it was possible for a man to know my body the way Brennon knows my body. Now I don't even want him touching my body."

"Oh shit, you're getting serious on me," Kaice replied.

"It's like that connection we've always had is fizzing out and I just can't figure it out. I don't know if it's him or me. Or both. I just don't want to hurt his feelings but it's just not working for me."

Skully cleared her throat. "Well, maybe you should find the words to tell him Storm. That's really none of our business and I don't think Bren would appreciate this conversation."

It had started off as a joke, Skully hadn't expected it to get serious and she wasn't interested in taking it any further.

"You're right. Let's nip it."

———

"How are you really, my girl?" Treasure asked.

"I've seen better days," Skully answered. "But I've

also seen worse. So, I can't complain."

"How are things at the shop?" Treasure continued with her line of questioning.

Treasure loved both of her daughters equally. Treasure looked after them both the same, but she always found herself a little more nurturing toward Skully because of everything she'd gone through.

"Good. I had to buy all new equipment, which was definitely a blow to the money I had going toward my move, but I'll get it back." Skully was certain.

"At least you have such a good friend in Law. That was really kind of him."

"Yeah. I'm still really trying to figure out how I feel about that. You know it seems a little too nice. You know me..." She took her longer fingernail and ran it across the tattoo across her hairline that read 'Never Trust.'

It wasn't quite on her face, but it was there. When you got close enough you saw it.

Treasure had never been a fan of it. She wasn't even against tattoos or anything like that, she just didn't want her daughter playing with her face. Some of these young people just went overboard.

"I get that, and you're right to not just go around trusting just anybody. Where you're wrong is sustaining this resentment towards all men because of the sins of one."

Skully let the words sink in. "I hear you. I hear everyone telling me I need to put myself out there again, but it's simply not that easy and there's simply nothing going on between me and Law."

"Okay and you're telling me you don't want there to be?" Treasure hiked her eyebrow. "Hell, the thoughts even crossed my mind. If I were just a couple years younger, aye, I'd take that fine specimen right off your hands."

"Just a couple?"

"Hey. You watch yourself." Her mother pointed at her with a chuckle. "On a serious note, I just want to see you happy my girl. One thing I've admired about you the most is your ability to always pick yourself up in the face of adversary. You're so strong. Stronger than you give yourself credit for at times, but don't let the world convince you that you always have to be. You can be vulnerable, ya know?"

"I know mama."

"I love you so much, beautiful. Whether I'm near or far I hope you know I'll get back here in 2.5 if you need me."

Skully would be sad to drop her mother at the airport the next day. She knew she was where she needed to be for her peace, but Skully just wished Treasure would move back.

If only she could snap her fingers and have it all back.

The family, her father, and her innocence before being dragged through the hell of a tumultuous relationship.

"I know. I love you, too."

"It was good to have you home ma." Storm sighed. "Even if it was just for a little while. You sure you can't stay longer? You did miss Thanksgiving." She tried guilting her.

"Yeah, you sure you can't stay?" Torrian asked. "Send Storm back in your place. Won't hear any complaints out of me."

"You leave my daughter alone Torrian." Treasure shook her head.

"I never did get your RSVP," Camile stated. "Will you be coming to the wedding?"

"Oh you'll be around my parts. You know ima make an appearance." Treasure answered.

"Good to know. Why didn't you RSVP? Why didn't anyone RSVP?" Camile huffed. "It's in the acronym. Respond!"

"If I'm correct it translates to, respond if you please."

"I think that's correct."

"Right, and that's why I didn't respond because I do whatever the hell I please." Treasure placed a hand on her hip.

"You're a mess lady." Storm shook her head.

"Brennon!" Treasure called. "Come on down here boy and get me to this airport!"

7

"*I*'m not going anywhere with him." Kaice shook her head in protest.

"Kaice. Don't be like that." Storm shook her head.

"No." Kaice continued to protest. "Uh uh, I'm not babysitting your twin brother tonight."

"Keep it up." Skully pointed with a threatening finger. "Get your friend." She told her sister.

Skully didn't want to go in the first place, she'd made a deal in exchange for them helping her move and she was holding up her end.

Storm only shook her head. "Leave her alone, but Skully you could've came a little harder."

Dressed in a pair of camo cargo-style joggers, a black bodysuit, and a pair of air max. Her hair was in a slick ponytail, and she wore a pair of hoops.

It wasn't that she didn't look cute, she just didn't

look ready for a date. Which was fitting, because Skully was not ready for a date.

"I mean you really letting your nuts hang." Storm joked with a chuckle.

"I think I see a lil Adam's Apple too." Kaice added and they both cackled.

Skully gave them both the middle finger.

"Come on, show some cleavage. Give em some boobies at least." Storm insisted.

"Boobies? Really?" Skully chuckled.

"Well, you ain't got titties so…"

"You know what! I'm bout sick of you both!"

Storm went into her closest before returning, "Here!" she tossed her a long sleeve black dress from her closet. "Looky, looky. It's long sleeve and comes past the knee. This should be suitable for you."

"But my ankles will be showing." Skully joked. "It's cold outside."

"Sometimes you have to sacrifice some things, you can't always be warm and cute. You got to choose sometimes."

"Well, of course that's not a problem for you. Hottie thottie."

"The cold never bothered me, anyway." Kaice sung the frozen lyric, sticking her tongue out.

"I don't even want to go to this stupid speed dating. This is childish."

"Please," Kaice replied. "Chile, we all know you are

hard-pressed for some hard peen. You can save that don't need a man mess for somebody else."

"You hush and go get us some drinks!" Storm directed. Put on the damn dress!" Storm demanded.

Skully knew there was no point and putting up an argument, she went into the bathroom and returned annoyed. "Happy?"

"Ecstatic." Storm responded sarcastically. Right on time for Kaice to enter the bedroom again, this time with glass shots and a bottle. "Now take a shot."

Kaice poured them up.

"To Skully finding her man!" Storm purposed the toast as they clinked glasses.

Skully took a small swig, but they weren't letting her get away with it.

"Uh uh, not the communion sip. Take that shit to the head!" Kaice encouraged.

"And another one!" Storm said just as she swallowed the first. "

———

By the time they made it to speed dating, Skully felt so good she forgot she didn't even want to be there.

The men were entertaining if she was being honest.

Skully was an hour in, and she'd laughed so hard her stomach hurt.

Law: You out for the night?

Skully: Nah, but I don't know how late I'll be. You waiting up for me?

Law: Should I?

Skully: Just wait up.

There wasn't any scenario where she planned on taking any of these men seriously, so yes, she was taking this like a joke.

"Well, how are you, baby? Don't just take a glance, come take a chance. Let me pull your chair out for you." He rushed around the table to help her.

Skully had to laugh. The man looked every bit of 40. Had the nerve to have a mouth full of golds.

"Damn girl, you looking like my future baby mama. Sit down, girl." He held out the chair for her. "Matter fact, stand back up, let me look at that thang one more time."

"Now why is it that a pretty girl such as yourself, doesn't have a man?" He asked.

"Actually, I do." She lied. "I'm just here to support a friend." She looked a couple tables down at Kaice.

"That's even better, baby. I'm just trying to be your sugar daddy."

"I don't think my boyfriend would appreciate me giving out his sugar."

"Quite frankly, I don't really care about your boyfriend, but you don't got to give up your sugar baby. You just might want to." He winked.

"Um, huh. What's the catch?" Skully crossed her arms.

"Pretty as you are, I know you got some pretty feet on you. I just want to get blessed with some pictures from time to time."

"Okay, excuse me, Sir. I'll be right back."

"That's alright with me too baby, because I love to watch you leave."

Skully shook her head as she walked over to Kaice. She greeted the man she was speaking with as she held onto the back of her chair, leaning in to speak into her ear. "I'm going to get out of here. You cool?"

"Oh, is he the one?" Kaice squealed. "I knew you'd find someone."

"Girl fuck you." Skully laughed. "That man is a heart attack away, from a VIP special at J P Porter." She referred to the local funeral home. "Ole freaky ass nigga got a foot fetish."

They cackled. Kaice's current date even chuckled. "You're wrong. You sure? There's a couple good ones left."

"I'm positive. I've hit too much liquor tonight, and it's starting to hit back. Besides, if I've got a man to get tonight, he's not here."

"Aw, you waited for me."

Skully was being carried inside the apartment.

Law recognized her brother- n -law Brennon from the night of the party.

"Here you sit down and eat this food you had me wait 40 minutes for." He sat Skully down onto the wooden dining room chair, taking the food out of the bag and placing it before her. "My bad-" he turned to Law. "I'm just walking up in your shit. Will you make sure she gets to bed straight?"

"I got her." Law confirmed.

"Preciate that." They shared a brief handshake before Brennon turned to give Skully's shoulder a brief squeeze. "Later sis. Call me in the morning."

"Bye Bren." She lifted her head like it was too heavy to hold up. "I'm really not drunk at all."

"Oh, I bet." He smirked pulling out the chair beside her.

"Don't throw up in my car Kaice." Brennon warned. "I see the way you going hard on that milk shake."

Kaice giggled. "I'm good. I'm good." She leaned her head against the window letting the nights air hit her. "It's just hot."

"You're just drunk." He corrected her shaking her head.

Apparently, Storm was responsible for getting Skully and Kaice home, but naturally since Strom wasn't feeling well, he became the Uber driver.

"I'm not, I'm not." Kaice denied.

Luckily, the ride to her house from Law's wasn't

long because he really wasn't convinced, she could hold it together for too much longer.

"Get out my car, Kaice. What you doing speed dating anyway, playa playa?" He teased.

"It's getting tired Bren, and so are these men out here." She shook her head. "Why is it so hard for me to find someone? All I'm asking is for love. I don't need the extra shit. I have my own money, car, job and house…"

"Yeah and you just want a man to pop in and fit right in where you want him to."

"Exactly!"

"But you know it don't work like that though. You want exactly what you want. When you want it. When not too long ago you were singing a whole different song."

"The thing is… I never stopped to think of how I'd truly feel sitting around watching all my friends find their soul mates, having kids and settling down and I'm still running around giving way too much to niggas who don't even deserve anything out of me."

One thing she could appreciate about Brennon was, he listened.

With Storm she always had to jump in whether it be just because she had something to say or to offer her "expert" advice.

Brennon just listened.

"I know I'm part of the problem I can own that, but I'm just exhausted at this point. Ready to throw in the towel. Why couldn't you just have a brother? Other than Torrian." She added leaning on his shoulder while laughing.

"You know... I always knew you and Storm were going to have this beautiful life together. From the very beginning you just always had your head on straight."

"Not always. Storm helped with that. A lot. I just always knew I loved her to death, and that was worth being the best version of myself for her. You'll bring that out of someone."

"We'll see." She sighed. "Anyway... that was a real sobering conversation." She laughed it off. "Thanks for the ride." She reached for the door handle. "By the way, I know you and Storm are going through whatever you're going through, but I know you'll work it out."

"Huh?"

"You know... sex isn't everything. I mean, maybe it's just the stress of trying for another baby. You know Storm's like hella dramatic. I mean I'm not trying to be all up in y'all bedroom, but I'm sure it's not that bad." Kaice looked over at Brennon and quickly saw the error of her ways. "It suddenly just got really hot again. So... I'm going to go. Thanks again Brennon!"

The quicker she got out of the car the better.

"You ever just sit back and think... Jack and the Box's menu is way too outrageous. Never ever should I be able to get an egg roll, taco, or fish sandwich from the same place." Skully shook her head.

"No," Law answered with a grin. "I can honestly say that's never crossed my mind."

"That's just me and my complex mind. I'm always thinking." She continued. "Over thinking at times. Like tonight showed me that. I was all up in arms about it, but what really could be so bad about going on dates and having a bunch of men vying for your attention."

"You really had me waiting up for you while you were on a date?"

"I did. Several actually! Lucky me, huh?"

"Lucky them." He corrected her. "Been at it going on two months and no such luck."

"You've never asked me on a date."

"I've done everything but spell out that I'm interest-ed." "Maybe you need to spell it then." She grinned.

"Maybe." He began clearing her spot for her. "I think I'll just call it for the night though."

"Are you sure that's what you want to do though?" Law swallowed the lump that formed in his throat, "That's what I should do."

"I didn't ask you what you should do." She hiked her dress up and straddled him in the chair. "I asked what you wanted to do." She brushed her lips against his.

He groaned as she rubbed her pelvis into him, still teasing with her lips.

She'd gon from not kissing the man to dry humping

him in the dining room. By the morning time she'd be beside herself.

He sucked in air as she continued to grind against his erection. "You can't keep doing that. Cause then ima…" he needed a minute. "Ima want to do something else."

"Good." The thin layer of her underwear was no match for the wetness between her legs.

She was the perfect balance between tipsy and alert. She knew exactly what she was doing and what she wanted.

Upon arrival, she hadn't had sex on her mind. The usual natural conversation that always flowed between the two would have been enough for her.

This was much better. Skully's entire body was ablaze. His touch to her skin was like fuel to a fire.

She leaned in to whisper in his ear, "I want to sit on it." She gave his ear a gentle bite that drove him crazy.

He pulled her head back and began kissing her with so much passion that it caught her by surprise.

It was the type of kiss that you felt all over. Skully's heart was pounding in her chest, her nose danced embracing the faint smell of his whisky breath and his lovely scent. She could bottle it up and probably come up on millions because every man could only wish to smell that good. It was almost more intoxicating than the liquor.

Law busied his hands as their tongues intertwined.

He locked his strong hands with hers and slid the condom he'd removed from his wallet into hers.

She stood up and stepped out of her lace underwear, while he watched her with lustful eyes.

In a squatting position Skully assisted him with unbuckling his belt, pulling down his pants followed by his boxer briefs.

His erect chocolate tool was just as mouthwatering as she anticipated.

Skully pinched the tip of the condom and placed it carefully behind her teeth using her tongue.

Then she did the unthinkable, lowering her mouth to the head of his penis and used her mouth to roll the condom over his full erection.

With her tongue, she made sure it was placed properly before pulling back and standing to her feet.

Using his shoulders for leverage she felt comfort in his strong arms around her waist as she sunk onto him slowly. Her mouth fell agape.

It had been a little over 3 years.

All she could do was relish in the feeling of him filling her. Up and down, her pace was slow to start as he held onto her for dear life.

His hands traveled up her dress as he began massaging her breast.

He closed his eyes as the sound of her moans filled his ear.

When he attempted to pull her dress over her head, she clenched herself around him, moving his hands away. She distracted him with her lips kissing him while riding him to oblivion.

With his strong arms, he held the chair down to keep them balanced, as he sent a slow, strong stroke upward that caused her head to fall back in awe.

He continued the slow and steady motion until her inner thigh began to shake and he began to pick up the pace. Until she had the most numbing release that gave her a sudden burst of energy.

Skully pushed him back in the chair regaining control, she could already tell he was right on the brink.

She leaned in to whisper, "Cum for me Lawrence."

His name on her tongue sounded like the sweetest song ever sung.

Biting down on her bottom lip she continued rotating her hips in slow, steady motions.

"Shitt!" He grunted as she felt the pulsating sensation just before he came.

They both needed a minute to catch their breaths. She let her face rest against the rise and fall of his chest as she continued releasing heavy breaths.

Until the chair gave up on them both leaving them both on the floor. The sounds of the people who lived under him hitting something against their ceiling could be heard as they both laughed hysterically.

———

"Good morning." Law entered the kitchen to find Skully cooking breakfast.

"Hi." She looked over her shoulder at him. "I'm making breakfast."

"I can see that. I appreciate it." He sat down at the table.

There was an elephant in the room.

"So..." they both attempted to speak at the same time.

"Go ahead." He encouraged.

"Last night, I was clearly inebriated. I don't take it back. I'm a grown ass woman, I'm not ashamed of what happen. It's just... it'd been like three years for me. So, I didn't expect my next time having sex to be on a whim one drunk night. I thought I'd be in a relationship and it'd be with someone I really care about."

"You don't care about me?" He challenged.

"I guess, I can't truthfully say that- can I? I'm rambling. I'm sorry. I do that when I'm nervous."

"I make you nervous still?" He pulled her closer to him. "Nothing's changed for me. Nothing."

Skully smiled to herself as he gave her-her space, retrieving orange juice from the refrigerator.

"I've been meaning to ask you something." He started. "There's a graduation celebration coming up. It's kinda a big deal. Mr. Dixon does everything big."

"Mr. Dixon... Like Elijah Dixon?" You didn't have to be involved in the law to know that name rung bells on and off the streets.

Dixon had dominated for years as one of the city's most prominent criminal lawyers, but his reach went beyond that. He had earned his stripes through the various high-profile cases he'd taken on and won. Went on to become a judge.

"He's my mentor," Law confirmed.

"Then you must be brilliant, because he's no small fry," Skully commented.

"And I'm no small fish."

Skully returned his smile.

"So, this is like a date? Am I being asked to be your date right now?"

"I mean, if you're not busy. I think you'd be proper arm candy."

"Nah, nah." She shook her head with a chuckle. "See, I really hit it off with Carl last night and he said I'm perfect sugar baby material... Just so you know, that's how he's coming? How you coming?"

"I think you know how I'm coming." He grinned. "I would really love if you would join me as my date."

"I would love to."

8

"You not about to get a turkey though." Torrian teased unconvinced Storm would be able to pull off her third strike in a row.

It was family bowling night, Storm was dominating for the second round in a row.

Being the competitor that she was, Storm was feeling herself.

"Bet." Storm nodded her head as she walked up to the lane. She did a false roll before walking back and moving up again.

The ball started off just enough to the left, to end up right in the middle and knock down all the balls.

"Gobble, gobble hoes!" Storm exclaimed.

"Y'all let this girl win two rounds." Kaice shook her head. "Not gon hear the end of it."

Everyone was having a good time. There were drinks going around, snacks, and good music.

"Everybody got one more round in them?" Camile asked.

"Last round." Torrian declared.

Kaice who was probably the drunkest of them all, went up to bowl and the ball ended up going backwards in the opposite direction.

They all died laughing.

"I got that on my story." Torrian laughed hysterically. "Went up there and became a whole Wii character."

"It's your turn Torrian." Storm said, still laughing.

"Let me see the video." Nari was still cracking up.

He handed over his phone before walking up to retrieve his ball. "I'm not playing no games this round." He pointed out Storm.

"Shaking in my boots." Storm joked.

Nari was cracking up all over again, after the video was finished it started over with his story from earlier.

A picture of them from brunch this morning, some highlight from a basketball game, a message on close friends, a group picture of all of them.... CLOSE FRIENDS?

Nari had to double back.

It would've gone right on by had it not been highlighted in green and it not occurred to her that she wasn't a part of his "close friends".

She looked up to see he was going for his second

turn, while she swiped up to see who had viewed that part of his story. There was one girl. The*Princess_Ariel*.

Ariel, huh? Close friends.

She closed the app and put the phone down upon his return beside her.

"It's your turn babe."

Nari's head was suddenly everywhere but bowling.

He smacked her ass as she went up for her turn, and she suddenly felt a whole lot less playful.

"Gutter ball!" Storm taunted.

When Nari came back to sit next to him he turned to her, "You good?"

"Yeah. I think I better get some food to soak up this alcohol."

"I got you, what you…"

"I'll get it." She cut him off.

———

"You just weren't going to tell me you had a birthday coming up." Skully placed a hand on her hip.

They had both had busy days, this was their first time seeing one another. She just so happened to be in the kitchen cooking when he got home.

"How did you-" He stopped himself when he saw the box on the counter containing the birthday cake. "Oh… that."

"Sorry. I'm nosy." Skully apologized. "Still doesn't negate the fact that you weren't going to tell me."

"My bad. It's just not a big deal to me." Law shrugged. "One year on family vacation in Florida we stopped at this bakery and we all fell in love with the owner Ms. Dorothy and her baked goods. Ever since then, my mama gets us a cake shipped in."

"That's sweet." Skully smiled. "Do you have any plans?"

"Nah, not really. It's not something I personally make a big deal about. Might end up chilling with the usual suspects."

That meant his brother and Lee.

Skully nodded her head.

"Alright Inspector Gadget, can I hop in the shower?"

"Hop away. You hungry?"

"Always."

"I got you."

———

"Hey babe." Storm leaned in to give him a quick kiss.

"Hey." Brennon didn't miss her eyes narrowing in on what he was doing on his laptop. "Don't even trip... I'm looking up stuff for Jeremiah's bachelor's party."

"Oh yeah." Storm rolled her eyes.

As if she and the girls weren't going to be just as turnt.

"What is that a problem?" He questioned.

"Not at all. I just don't understand why men have to

go all crazy in strip clubs like you don't lay next to a beautiful woman with a banging body every night."

"Y'all gon have y'all fun and you got me, so same difference."

"Not exactly. Y'all like to make a pastime of the strip club and you can miss me it ain't about the wings."

"Is this really an argument right now?" He released an exasperated sigh.

"Chill out. I'm not trying to argue with you right now." She held up her hand taking offense. "If you like it, I love it."

There it was. Brennon knew what that meant, and she did not love it.

"Maybe I should take a note out of your book and start to frequent the strip club more often."

"Hmm, seeing as to how I can't please you that might work out for you, huh?"

Storm's face turned beet red.

"But you talk about that with everybody but me."

Storm cleared her throat, shifting uncomfortably. "Brennon... I'm sorry..."

"Don't be. I would never put you out there like that, but it doesn't even matter when we just gon sweep it under the rug like all of our other issues."

Now Storm was on the defense. "Wait, so all of a sudden our marriage is in shambles because we're not having sex."

Brennon let out a heavy sigh. "You tell me. You're the one with the problem."

"Now I got problems. Wow. Keep it up. I'm oh so wet right now." Storm said sarcastically. "This is really helping."

"Aye, I'm really trying my hardest not to argue with you right now but stop playing with me!"

"Nobody's playing anything. If anything, I was trying to spare your feelings. I didn't know how to tell you that."

"Then just tell everyone else but me. Real smooth. Way to go."

"I didn't tell everyone I told Skully and Kaice. I know Skully didn't rat me out so Kaice looking hella sus right now."

"Why are you trying to turn this on everyone but you?"

"What am I in trouble? I'm not turning this on anyone. Neither of us wants to argue. So, let's just not."

"End of discussion because you said so. Sounds about right."

"What do you even want from me, Bren?!?" Storm threw her hands up. "Besides sex!"

"Sex was never the point, but its dead."

"You're still up?" Law poked his head inside her room.

"Picked the wrong time to start binge-watching Law & Order," Skully replied.

"Understood." He nodded. "You up for company?"

She lifted her blanket so he could join her underneath when he joined her on the bed.

Skully immediately found comfort lying against Law's chest. A warm feeling came over her.

A moment of silence passed between them.

"Tell me about your sister," Skully demanded.

"No." There was no hesitation.

There wasn't even wiggle room. No way to get anything confused- he didn't want to talk about it.

Unfortunately for him, Skully didn't care, "What was she like?"

Skully had come to know him and his boundaries better, and she had no issue disregarding them and overstepping them.

It was one of those things that he recognized about her and despised at times.

"Skully." He warned with her eyes.

Skully sat up, crossing her legs so that she could look him directly in his face. "It's obviously something you don't want to talk about, but you know you probably should. When you're ready, I would like to hear about her though."

"There're articles out there. Read them." He added. "Why are you so interested, anyway?"

"I won't pretend to know what your sister went through. I can only speak from my experience. I'd like to think her situation wasn't as ugly as mine, but you know…. You never know."

There was the longest pause. Skully could admit she

could overstep some boundaries, but the look of disdain on his face told her she might've gone too far.

He ran his hand over his face. "I can't put myself in the position of knowing exactly what my sister went through because she didn't tell me, but I can only blame myself because I should've been there. She shouldn't have had to come to me because I should've just been there!"

His eyes flashed with a passion that masked the tears that welled in his eyes.

She rubbed his shoulder comfortingly. "Sometimes we as people convince ourselves that we're burdening the people who care about us by introducing our problems."

In getting him to open up about his sister, she found herself opening up old wounds of her own.

There was a time when the topic alone would send her on a whole downward spiral.

Now she was past it if there was ever such a thing.

"Tell me about him." He was flipping the script on her.

Skully wasn't sure she was ready for this vulnerability with him, but hell she had brought it on herself.

"He tried to kill my confidence, my self-esteem, my sense of self, my independence, and even tried to kill my relationship with the people closest to me. When that didn't work, he tried to kill me."

He released a sharp breath. She wasn't his sister, but she was somebody he found himself growing to care about. Regardless of who "he" was, it struck a nerve.

"Sounds like a whole bitch." He finally spoke.

"Yes, and he's no longer breathing," Skully stated. "And I'm so thankful that I am."

Another moment of silence passed before he got to talking. "She was annoyingly happy all the time. You could just never believe it was possible for someone to be that happy all the time, but then it rubbed off on you. She was just such a good person, and that doesn't get praised enough."

It was clear he had more to get off his chest, so he could take as much time as he needed to process his thoughts.

"Good people can get caught up in bad things. It doesn't matter that she smoked weed on occasions. It doesn't matter that she didn't always make the best decisions. It doesn't matter that she wasn't perfect! She was simply a good person, my little sister, and she deserved better."

Skully understood where he was coming to the fullest.

The critiquing of the victim was something Skully could never wrap her head around.

"I was so wrapped up in all of my school shit, my own shit. I buried my baby sister with the burden of knowing I wasn't there for her the way I should've been. When I should've been."

"That's just the hurt talking."

"Yeah, well… that's enough talking." He planted a kiss on her neck, then lifted her chin with his fingertip to bring her lips closer to his.

"Oh my gosh!" Camile squealed. "This is even better than I thought."

Camile had successfully picked out bridesmaid's dresses that looked great on them all, from online. She was patting herself on the back.

Her whole wedding party was present, including her mother Wilma- who was mainly just minding her business.

"Y'all look so beautiful." She wiped mock tears. "I did that!"

"Um huh. They look alright." Kaice teased.

"Sorry Kaice. I really didn't think you expected to be a bridesmaid." Camile replied. "Still love you though. You and Nari are honorary bridesmaids."

"It's all good. I just hope there are some eligible bachelors at this wedding." Kaice shrugged.

"Girl swear she always on the prowl." Skully shook her head with a grin.

"You know this."

"Come on in here and eat these good appetizers I whipped up." Camile ushered them into the kitchen. "Aht-aht-aht… out of those beautiful gowns first my pretties."

"You know I'll introduce you to anybody worth-while and warn you who to stay away from." Camile continued the conversation, as the girls trickled back into the kitchen from getting changed. "You know, girl code."

"Speaking of…" Storm cleared her throat. "Kaice, I don't really appreciate you running back our private conversations to my husband."

"I could say the same about you calling me out in front of everyone here, but please do fill me in on what you're talking about."

"I'm just saying I'm having conversations I wasn't ready to have with my husband about something I trusted you with. As my girl, I talk to you about personal matters such as my sex life at what point did that come up in conversation between you and my husband?"

"Hold on now…" Camile placed her hand on her hip.

"Whoa, you're turning this into something that it wasn't. It was an innocent conversation, I slipped up. Obviously, Brennon felt a way about it, my bad. I'm sorry."

"Yes. He's being hella sensitive about it. It'll pass." Storm brushed it off. "What's so wrong about me voicing my frustrations to people who I talk to about everything?"

"Now you wrong." Wilma butted in. She was sitting at her table, already getting into her rotel. "Don't do that. Dismissing that man's feelings in ways you would have a fit if he did yours."

Kaice smirked. While she loved her friend dearly, she still didn't appreciate Storm's approach. She could appreciate the support from someone unbiased-pointing out Storm's wrongs.

"I'm not dismissing his feelings."

"I don't know Storm men don't take it light when they not laying the pipe." Camile shook her head. "That's a blow to the ego."

"All I said was something was different between us. I'm just not satisfied right now, not like I said I never was."

"Either way, you wouldn't want him going around to his boys telling them that you're a lousy lay," Wilma told her. "Think about that."

"Well, I'm not." Storm was on the defense.

"I'm not coming for you. What if that man is just as unsatisfied, and is just sparing your feelings? It wasn't right for you to discuss that man in such a manner when you haven't done so to his face."

"Brennon's a good man..." Kaice began.

"I know that, that's why I'm married to him." Storm cut her off. "I don't need you telling me about my husband."

"Well, if you would have let me finish... I was only going to say Brennon's just coming from a place of hurt and y'all are both so caught up in y'all feelings that there's all type of miscommunication going on."

"Thanks for all this marital advice, I assure everyone Brennon and I are just fine."

―――――――

"Excuse me, sir."

Law recognized the voice before he even laid eyes on her. She always had the sweetest voice to him. Especially when she was calling out his name.

"I cannot let you take the last Sicilian pizza," Tatum told him.

California kitchen pizza was one of those places Tatum had put him on to.

"Won't fight you on that." Law gave it up with little fight.

Not much different from the way Tatum effortlessly got her way in their relationship.

An awkward moment passed before Tatum said, "So, we gon act like we don't go way back? No hug."

"My bad. I just wanted to be respectful. Thought your man might be around here somewhere." He looked around jokingly before leaning in to give her a hug.

"Hm." Tatum exhaled. "You smell good. You always do."

"You look good." He complimented her. "Always do."

There wasn't a person with working eyes that would deny Tatum's outward beauty.

Tatum's skin was rich and chocolate. She had the prettiest dark brown eyes and a high cheek-boned smile. His favorite feature of hers was the thick, beautiful mane she wore in various styles, today a beautiful puff atop of her head.

"And I don't know what man you're talking about, but if I have a secret admirer out there somewhere send him my way."

Law nodded his head. "I never know. You didn't seem so single the last time."

Tatum rolled her eyes. "It was a fling. I'm so single, can you say the same?" She challenged.

"I can."

"Not what I heard."

"You heard some things, I heard some things. We should both know better than to trust the grapevine for accuracy."

"Then let me go right to the source with it. Who's the new girl?"

"No one of interest to you. I don't have a girl-friend, that's all you need to know." Law clarified. "How have you been holding up though?" He changed the subject.

"Better than most. You?" She asked.

"Good," Law answered. "Almost to that finish line, you know."

"I know, and I couldn't be any prouder Law school. Congratulations."

"Thank you."

"Well, I saw you just thought I'd be my usual bothersome self." She grinned.

"Glad you did." Law nodded. "It was good seeing you."

"Good to be seen," Tatum responded. "Here." She handed the pizza back to him.

"You're good." He shook his head in protest.

"I insist. Consider it an early birthday gift." She was already backing away. "Think of me every bite."

He chuckled shaking his head, "Bye Tatum."

"I don't know... His birthday is tomorrow, and I just feel like I should do something a little special for him right?" Skully inquired.

"WRONG!" Storm blurted obnoxiously. "Why you acting like you owe that man something?"

"I am being all weird, huh?" Skully replied. "It's just... I've never lived with a man."

"And? He's still not your man."

"That's a valid point, but just as you suggest I don't owe him anything he didn't owe me anything when he so kindly opened up his home to me."

"Yeah and I know you've been feeling all extra kind since you opened up your legs to him, but don't go getting all dickmitized. Don't be the non-girlfriend doing girlfriend duties thinking it's going to earn you brownie points."

"Alright, I think I've taken enough of a verbal beating. I'm off here since you just woke up and chose violence today."

"Yeah, yeah. I got to go cook anyway." Storm stated.

"What are you cooking?"

"Hamburger helper. Brennon's in the doghouse girl. I ain't gon starve him but he ain't eating 5-star either."

Skully could only laugh while shaking her head to herself. "I don't know how that man puts up with it."

———

The next morning Law's birthday was the first thing that came to Skully's mind.

She could take heed to her sister's warnings and celebrates a friend's birthday simultaneously.

Contrary to popular belief, she knew her place.

While she wasn't going to make a big deal of his birthday, she was still going to at least be good company for him.

After brushing her teeth and washing her face, she went to peek her head into the room. To find him not there.

She opted to shoot him a text and go have breakfast herself.

———

Law was drunk as hell by 12pm.

First thing in the morning his mother and Larry had ambushed him.

"I know how you get son, and you'll go into your little bubble of seclusion." His mother had said. "So, let's go!"

She was right to do so, and she definitely boasted his spirits.

It was downhill from there.

Skully: Happy Birthday! Hope you're having a good day & you're in good spirits. See you later.

"So, now all of a sudden you not feeling Skully?" His brother Terrance turned up his face.

"I didn't say all that." Law denied. "I'm just saying this isn't really my speed. I'm used to moving things way slower."

"Yeah, yeah. That sounds good, but we both know the truth." Terrance remarked. "You were all in about a week ago. Then you ran into Tatum at the store, now your heads all fucked up."

"Oh, Lord." His father, Jeffery chimed in. "Now son, I don't know what love spell, voodoo type shit that girl done put on you but every time she comes around all your good God-given sense goes out the window."

"Yeah whatever."

"Anyway, I like the Skully girl. So, don't mess it up."

"You don't even know her. Only reason you're saying that is because you don't like Tatum."

"Exactly. So, don't mess it up."

Terrance had long ago taken a step back from interjecting himself into his brother's on and off, up and down relationship. Opposed to allowing it to further cause tension in their relationship as it had years ago, he just opted to not concern himself with it, but there were some things he had to get off his chest.

"Look, you have a thing about you where you treat women like they're at your disposal. Including Tatum." It was difficult to even halfway come to Tatum's defense. "This back-and-forth y'all been doing over all these years, it's only because she's willing to stick around but you've done this with every woman. As soon as shit gets too deep, too real. You're out. You telling me that's not what you doing right now?"

If Law weren't playing his own defense, he would have to admit that Terrance was right.

He was pushing her away.

It was different when they were just friends, and he was just enjoying her company. It was even different when he let her move in, he honestly didn't mind her moving in. He wasn't even lying when he said the sex hadn't changed anything in his head.

Keeping her at a safe distance had always been the plan. Now he was learning more about her and talking to her about his sister.

"This really you right now?" Law almost couldn't believe it. "Is that not the pot calling the kettle black?"

"We're not talking about me, we're talking about you. And the difference between me and you is I don't make relationships of my commitment issues. I'm real about my shit and I'm real single. I'm real adamant about being single until I feel like I'm ready to settle down. You on the other hand, claim to be this all-around good, relationship guy and you get in the relationship, and it's fucked up from the start because of the baggage that you bring into them. The only difference is I own it, but I'm the bad guy!"

"Talk to him son." Jeffery encouraged.

"What is this, a birthday intervention?"

"It's what you need to hear if you don't want to make the same mistakes I made with your mama."

"Now we talking about you and ma?"

"Nah we not doing that." Terrance shook his head. "We get to talking about what you did to my mama that's when I have to put hands on you."

That's how their relationship went. Terrance and Law were able to accept and see Jeffery for who he was which is why they didn't have that same resentment they did as kids.

"Alright, let's get a round of shots!" Jeffery blurted out.

———

"This is a surprise." Storm commented as her sister entered her room.

Skully wouldn't expect anything less than her sister being 100% obnoxious, when she was 100% right.

Skully climbed into the bed with her. "He never showed?" Storm concluded.

"Nope," Skully answered. "Even worse, I was going to let him have his cake and my cookie."

Storm released a dramatic gasp.

"Now we're going to have his cake." Skully opened the box. "And some liquor."

"You stole his cake." Storm laughed. "This shit looks good too."

"How disappointing that must be. To have to keep those cookies in the jar."

"Yeah, I've been holding back since that first time. I just didn't want things to turn into some sort of friends with benefits bullshit when I thought we were building something solid. Now I'm not even sure about the friendship part."

"Aww look at you all flustered and in lust."

"You're not helping." Skully shook her head.

"Sorry I just don't see you like this often it's kinda cute, because I think you really like him. Nonetheless, you're just thinking with your kitty kat right now. Give it a couple of days you'll be back to the heartless heffa I know and love."

"I'll drink to that."

$\mathcal{S}$kully looked through the peep hole cautiously, her face scrunched up in confusion as she opened the door.

"Ugh hi." Skully greeted the girl awkwardly.

"Oh hey." She appeared to be just as confused to see Skully answering the door. "I'm Tatum."

"Skully." She was still waiting for an explanation.

"Skully. What a unique name."

Bitch. Skully was not feeling her whole vibe. "Can I help you?" She cleared her throat.

"Is Law around?"

"No," Skully answered dryly.

He wasn't. Hadn't been answering the phone either.

Skully stood awkwardly as the girl pulled out her cellphone to call who she assumed to be him. She was right. Even worse, he answered- for her.

Skully could only hear her end of the conversation,

which was enough to drive her crazy as she stood there giggling and carrying on. Laying it on thick.

"I guess I should've called but you know me... I pull up." More giggles. "We have to catch up some other time. You know how we love..." her voice dipped to a lower, sultry tone. "To catch up." She finished her sentence. "I look forward to it. See you soon." She ended the call. "Well, I'm sorry to have bothered."

Skully doubted that very seriously.

Her smug facial expression said otherwise.

Skully regretted not just shutting the door in her face to begin with.

"I'm sure." Skully crossed her arms. "For future references, maybe don't show up to our apartment this late. To you know, avoid something like this." Skully killed her with a smug grin of her own.

"Ha!" Of course, Tatum's antics continued. With her dramatic laughter. "You spend the night? Cute."

"No, I live here." Skully corrected her. The logistics didn't matter. The girl was truly trying to play her, and she wasn't letting up.

"Yeah sure. When and if Law tells me, he has a problem with when I choose to come over, I may stop. Until then, you can have several seats."

"Well, I'll be sure that we have that discussion and I'm sure he'll relay that message."

"You think? Let me explain something to you, I've been around for years you've been around for months. Don't think for one second you could EVER have one up on me." That had escalated quickly. Suddenly the nice-nasty act was dropped, and Tatum was just being outright nasty.

"Bless your little heart." Skully grinned. "I've ruffled your little feathers in minutes and Law's in months. Clearly. How long was it before you moved in?"

"Just don't get comfortable sis," Tatum remarked. "Daddy always comes home, but if it makes you feel better, I'll let you playhouse."

Skully was boiling on the inside. Why was she arguing with this gorgeous woman over a man who she had no claims to?

They didn't have a title they didn't have anything.

Here she was staying at his house, which had never felt sillier than now.

"You have a nice night." Tatum pranced away feeling like she'd had the last word, and therefore- she won.

"What the fu-" The box he tripped over interrupted his sentence.

In fact, half the living room was covered in cardboard boxes. He followed the sounds of Summer Walker and Jhene Aiko all the way to Skully's room where she was singing her heart out.

As the song came to an end Jhene's soft voice came in heavy with another song that let him know he was up shits creek.

"The feelings have been mutual, I'm ready to let you know. Don't wanna see you no more..."

Even as he hovered over her, looking right down at her she paid him dust.

It wasn't until he walked over to her speaker and turned it down.

"Can I help you with something? Want this playlist too?" She arched her eyebrow. "I call it niggas ain't shit."

Law tucked his hands in his pockets. "What's all this about? You weren't even going to tell me? Why Skully?"

"Because it's time." She declared.

"You found a place?"

"Doesn't matter. I'm a big girl. I'll figure it out. I've overstayed my welcome here and I'm not comfortable making people feel uncomfortable in their own home..."

"Where's all this coming from? I never said you had to leave or that you make me uncomfortable. So, when'd you come to this conclusion?"

"Probably somewhere within the two days, you didn't bother coming home. I mean I wasn't exactly waiting up, but I was expecting to see you for your birthday. Friend." She hissed the word like he wasn't even deserving of the title.

Skully didn't return home until late, having had a busy day of work. She was completely prepared to give him the coldest shoulder and was certain a bs apology or excuse was to come. However, she got neither. She didn't even get the luxury of his presence.

That was night two of Skully looking like a dumbass.

Law ran his hand over his face. He knew he'd fucked up. "You don't have to do this." He let out an exasperated sigh. "I never said I wanted you to leave."

"Your actions said everything your mouth didn't. Look me in my eyes and tell me I'm wrong. Tell me I'm not the reason you haven't been home."

He could tell her that, but it would only be partially true.

His being in his own head about her had been more than enough to keep him away for days.

"I'm sorry."

She let out a frustrated sigh, "What are you even apologizing for?"

"I hurt your feelings obviously. I'm never trying to do that. So, I'm sorry."

"I don't need your apology and I don't need to take up any more of your space. Give me until tomorrow morning and I'll be out of it."

"Look if you're really ready to go I'm not gonna stop you." He instantly regretted not choosing better words. "Listen…" he continued. "My initial offer remains the same, you can stay here as long as you need. I can't even lie and pretend like putting some space between us these last couple of days wasn't my intention, but you can't imagine how fucked up my heads been having you here."

"Sorry I've become such a problem for you."

No matter what he said he couldn't get it right.

"It's not you. It's everything happening between us that we're not talking about. I've never felt this way this fast about anyone."

"Aww I get it."

Finally. He could breathe a sigh of relief after putting his foot in his mouth since the moment he entered her room.

"You were avoiding a "what are we conversation." She concluded. "You bitched up at the mere thought of commitment."

Just like that, back at square one.

"You're really going to be this much of a hard-ass right now? When I'm trying to be vulnerable with you."

"You want a cookie for that? Being vulnerable? Something women do every day, despite all the bullshit men put us through while claiming to care about us. If that's where we're going with this let's go ahead and wrap this up. So I can pack this up and be on my way."

"Skully... you're not even giving me a chance."

"A chance to what?"

"Look, I care about you. Really care about you." He emphasized. "As a friend and as someone, I want to be with. I want to be a friend to you but I'm trying to be way more than that too."

"Then you're really, really going to have to make me

believe it. Saying it just isn't enough. The last person I let in ruined me. Why would I expect any more out of anyone else? That's why I'm a hard ass because I got to be."

"Skully. It won't happen again. Please stay. Not just because I know I fucked up, just because I want you here."

"Okay."

"Okay?"

"Don't let it happen again."

"I swear on my life I won't."

She believed him. Whether it was, because she just wanted to, or because he was speaking truth, it was to be determined.

"Okay."

———

Nari was withering.

She wasn't the type to play her hand. Which meant behaving as if everything was perfectly normal, despite her inner turmoil.

Since the bowling alley, she'd been building her case. So far, she hadn't found anything that could confirm or deny cheating.

She couldn't find her in his phone, not a trace of messages or DMs between the two. Just the close friends.

Were they talking in code? A strategic cheater was

even worse. That made this feel like a continuous thing, not an *oops,* but something he was actively pursuing and covering up.

From what Nari could see of her page by way of her friend befriending her on Insta, her page was a bottomless gallery of pictures Torrian wouldn't approve of her posting.

Nari didn't have hate in her blood, so she could admit the girl was pretty and her shape was nice.

"Damn baby, you didn't cook me anything?" Torrian had the nerve to be offended.

Every time she looked at him, she got heated all over again.

"Nope." She said blankly. "And I'm also watching this, so please don't come up in here talking to me."

She could be doing absolutely nothing, and she still wouldn't want him talking to her in that moment.

"Okay." He took a heavy sigh. "What did I do?"

"I don't know. Did you do something Torrian?" She gave him her full attention.

"I mean the way you acting…"

"I'm just acting like someone who would really like to eat my food and watch my show free of interruption."

"Okayy… you must be going through your shit right now. So, ima let you have it."

He started to walk away and Nari was fine with that, but of course, he doubled back.

"I just always got to walk on eggshells with you. We

can be so good and then you just flip the switch. I don't even know how to handle you..."

"Then don't." She shrugged. "Just don't." her voice cracked.

Nari couldn't explain why she was getting emotional. She didn't know why they were arguing so much lately.

The most crucial thing, she didn't know that he wasn't cheating on her.

Torrian's wordless response was to simply give her a hug.

He didn't always know what to say, and sometimes he'd put his foot in his mouth. On the other hand, he knew she needed him, and there was nowhere else he wanted to be.

———

"You decided to leave, anyway?" The sight of Skully wheeling the suitcase down the hall made his chest feel tight.

The things this woman was doing to him, he couldn't explain.

He wasn't lying when he said he cared about her. He also wasn't sure what that meant for them. In any regard, caring about someone, their well-being, and their happiness felt like one of those things you treasure.

One of those things that could transform a friendship into something else, because maybe he wanted to be her happiness.

That's what scared him.

"Ugh yeah." She answered.

He let out a heavy sigh. "Can't say I don't wish I didn't talk you out of it."

"Only for a couple of days." Storm explained. "I have a conference to go to."

"Then you'll be back?"

"Maybe."

"Can you at least call me when you make it?"

"Maybe."

It wasn't going to be as simple and easy as a conversation.

Even if she could trust that he really cared about her, she didn't trust him with his ex and that was enough to make her fall all the way back.

"Are you still going to be able to make it to the graduation party?" He questioned.

"Maybe."

That was enough for him, but even though she was playing games he'd started them. He shouldn't have tried to run.

He used his hand to grab her gently by the neck, pulling her into him.

The smell of the mint gum on her breath teased his nose as he held her face close to his.

"Take care of what you got to take care of then come home." He spoke with authority. "To me." He added before leaning in teasing her with his lips that he brushed up against hers.

The way his beard tickled against her chin caused butterflies to dance in her stomach.

Suddenly he pulled away. "I've held you up long enough. Be safe. Call me." He demanded.

Skully would have been lying if she said she didn't like that.

"Mama!!!" Nari called as she entered the house.

"I'm in the kitchen!" Her mother Shanice called from the kitchen.

"Hey lady." Nari walked in.

"You're just in time for red beans and rice, and cornbread," Shanice explained.

"Oh, I don't need it." Nari denied shaking her head. "Feel like all I been doing is eating. Look at me mama."

"My little thickums. You got your lil woman weight. Looks good on you."

Nari chuckled taking a seat. "Go ahead and make me a plate."

"Girl I was already on it. Here."

Shanice and Nari had always been close, most people said their relationship was more like sisters than mother and daughter.

It was just Nari and her older brother Damitri, who

had taken on the role of *man of the house.* Nari was used to being babied.

"How's my son?" She asked.

"He's good."

"But he's not here, and y'all be attached at the hip, so what's wrong?"

"Nothing that I know of, but you know how you're always telling me I'm always looking for something to be wrong."

"Because you do…"

"Yes, well… I don't know if that's what's going on because my gut feeling is telling me something else."

"Where is this coming from though? You two were just all good. I'm not understanding."

"Ma… Just believe me when I say I have my doubts and I have my reasons."

"Then that's what it is," Shanice stated like it was facts. "I always tell you, go with your gut. So, do we have a problem?"

"I don't know mama." Nari let out a heavy sigh. "I mean I'm definitely going to find out, but it's like once again I'm looking for the bad when everything's going good. And I know I'm a lot for Torrian to handle."

"Would you rather be, hard to handle or easy to play with?"

"You're right, you're right. But I also know I have a terrible habit of projecting the trauma I have from living through your toxic relationship, onto my own."

Shanice let out a heavy sigh. It was a tough pill to

swallow knowing that she'd contributed to her child's trauma.

Her ex was mentally and verbally abusive. Any way he could tear Shanice down, he did just that.

Cheated on her throughout the entire 10 years they were together. All Shanice ever knew was him belittling her, making her to blame for his infidelity and after so long of him telling her how no one else would want her-she believed it.

All Nari ever knew was her mother hurting and crying, but never leaving.

Nari vowed to never be that weak with anyone. Sometimes she felt like she was too hard for her own good, but it was hard not to be.

"Baby let me tell you this. You are 20 years old. There's never a good time to be pressed over any man, but now is especially not it."

"Even if it's a man who I love?"

"Honey, you still got a lot to learn about love. You are young, beautiful, and smart as hell. You have so much going for yourself and so much ahead of you. If Torrian doesn't realize that he's got the crème de la crème that's his loss."

Nari smiled. "Thanks mama. I love you."

"I love you more girly."

10

"*I* want to start by expressing my gratitude for being able to host such a dope event." Rochelle was a tattoo artist Cali born and raised whose name rung bells as one of the elites in the tattoo world.

"It's important to me as a black woman first and foremost to appreciate that this year's number of women artists triple last year's." She paused to allow the applause that followed. "So much talent in the room. So much beautiful art. Yes, art. For some reason the art I choose to ink on my body seems to be labeled trashy, or tacky. And we as tattoo artists seem to be on the low totem pole of art, which puts a bad taste in my mouth because I'm serious about my shit." This brought some laughter.

"So, I want to welcome everyone and thank all the artists that are here because there's a little bit of art in all of us. Welcome to this year's annual Art Villain

Convention, don't forget all your donations help. This year's proceeds go to YBEF Young Black Entrepreneurs Foundation. Thank you."

The crowd erupts in applause.

The convention was everything Skully expected and more.

The room was littered with unique, vibrant artwork from all the different artists. Some of the most elite tattoo artists from all over filled the room.

Skully had been hard at work all day. It was like a marathon- nonstop. She didn't mind one bit, because she was doing what she loved.

"Alright bae. You need anything before I head out?" Torrian questioned.

"Nah. I'm coo. I'm chilling." Nari answered. "You going to your brothers?"

"Yeah, but I don't know how late I'll be," Torrian explained.

"Hm. Maybe I should come then. Keep Storm company. I know she's not into sports and you like to hog up her husband." She chuckled.

It was a test. She looked over at him, waiting for his response.

"I mean, yeah. That's coo. You ready?"

"I'm just messing with you. Go have your fun, but not too much fun without me. Then come home and have some fun with me." She grinned, leaning in to give him a kiss.

"Oh yeah? That's how you feeling?" He kissed her again. "I love you."

"I love you, too." She smiled all the way until he walked out of the room.

Lying ass.

"All done." Skully smiled.

"That wasn't as bad as I thought." Zuri used the mirror to view the trail of music notes behind her ear. "And I love it. Thank you for squeezing me in."

"Of course. You just don't know how I'm fan-girling in my head." Skully responded.

Zuri was an R&B artist who had gained popularity over the last year after releasing her first EP. Now her album was on the way, and her star power was increasing.

She was also from the city.

Skully was happy to see anybody make it big from Louisville, Kentucky. Especially if they were black, a black woman was a bonus.

Skully would be a forever fan.

"Well, when I heard about you, I had to come show my support."

Zuri had shown her nothing but love. In addition to the tat, she'd purchased one of her exclusive pieces and not for cheap.

"It's much appreciated."

"It's much deserved. You in your own shop?"

"Not just yet, but when the time's right. For sure."

"Well, I don't want to be intrusive, but take it from me. As long as you're in your own head, the time will never be right. It's okay to take your time just don't get stagnant."

Skully wouldn't usually be as receptive of someone she'd known a day having so much to say, but they had just clicked and had a real ass conversation.

"Thank you. I feel like I needed to hear that."

"Me too. Keep in touch? Next times got to be in your own shop though."

"Next time."

"What y'all down here doing?" Storm descended the basement steps.

Brennon really had turned it into his own. Storm could see it being hard to come up at times. Hell, he had his own bathroom, bar, and kitchen area.

He damn near had a whole separate house.

"Watching the game." Torrian answered.

"I didn't even know you were down here." She told Kaice.

Her friend was basically a beautiful ass tom boy.

Sometimes she wondered if she preferred the boy's company over the girls.

"Hey sis." Kaice greeted her.

"No invite though?" Storm asked. "I like sports too."

"No you don't."

"You're right I don't." She walked over to Brennon to give him a kiss. "I'm going to the gym with the girls."

"Camile got y'all in pre-wedding boot camp, huh?" Jeremiah questioned.

"Ha. Yeah."

"Alright y'all have fun," Brennan remarked.

"Yeah right. I'll be back, though. Jelani's out like a light."

"Bet."

———

"What are you going to do?" Storm wondered.

"What would you do if you found out Brennon was cheating?" Nari inquired.

"End up on an episode of snapped." Storm replied.

"Hold up, whatever happen to innocent until proven guilty?" Camile questioned. "You could be getting yourself all worked up for no reason."

Nari had filled them in on all the details. From that first night at the bowling alley when she'd discovered Torrian's secret "close friends", until now.

Tonight had tipped Nari right over the edge.

When she looked on Torrian's Instagram and saw

the location of the hotel, only for *ThePrincess_Ariel* to see, her heart sunk to her stomach.

It never bothered her that Torrian would spend so much time with Brennon and their friend group because most of them were in committed relationships. If anything, she thought the men could be a positive influence on him.

Now that everything was coming undone, it appeared to Nari her unwavering trust for him made it perfect for him to do extracurriculars with ease and for it to go unnoticed.

"What if he doesn't come? The whole thing might not be what you think it is. He was chillin when I left."

"Sounds like an alibi to me. Would you tell me if you knew something I didn't?"

At this point Nari was questioning everything and everyone.

"Nari, Torrian would know better than to let me find out he was cheating on you. I'd kill him myself."

"What if he doesn't come for hours?" Camile questioned from the backseat.

She was like an anxious little kid. Camile really wasn't sure how she got dragged into this mess. Her mind had really been on the gym, she had her sweat belt on and everything.

"Then it's a muthafuckin stakeout." Nari stated.

"It's a stakeout then." Storm loved her brother-n-law no matter how much they went at it.

However, Nari was like the little sister of the crew.

If he were cheating, the woman in her would have to be on Nari's side.

"I personally would just like to know if there's steak in this stakeout." Nari turned and looked to her with fire in her eyes. "Aight, ima let y'all have it. I'll just sit back here and be quiet."

Moments of tense silence passed.

They were all on edge.

"I don't know ladies." Camile shook her head from the backseat, breaking the silence. "I mean… Let's stop and think about this, do you really wanna know?"

"Hell yeah. The fuck I look like?" Nari questioned.

"Mario Winans apparently." Storm piggy-backed.

She was laughing now, but things were about to get real unfunny if she were right.

———

The sound of Storm's phone ringing for the second time in a row finally jolted her out of her sleep.

"Hello." She answered the phone drowsily.

"Where you at babe?" Brennon asked.

She glanced at the time on her screen and realized over 2 hours had passed. To her left, Nari was knocked, and Camile was stretched across the backseat.

"I fell asleep at Nari's. The gym kicked my ass."

"I figured that."

"Only because I was benching 200 and ran 10 miles."

"You don't even believe that ya damn self."

They both laughed at that. "Everybody still there?"

"Nah. Kaice and Torrian left a lil minute ago."

"Alright. I'll be home shortly. I don't want to drive while I'm too sleepy."

"Call me when you heading home. Love you."

"Love you too."

After ending the call, she attempted to wake the girls. When neither of them bulged she turned the music all the way up which got their attention.

"We got to go home. It's late and I'm tired, and there's no Torrian in sight."

"Nah, he's not getting off that easy." Nari scanned the parking lot with her eyes before stepping out of the car.

Camile and Storm followed suit. In pursuit of his car.

They searched around the parking lot full of cars, using the flashlight from Nari's phone.

Storm was first to notice it, she didn't say anything at first. She was stunned to silence.

A black charger with tinted windows and U of L plates stuck out like a sore thumb.

When Nari saw for herself that was all the ammunition she needed as she entered the hotel on a mission.

"Hello, how are you?" Nari greeted the receptionist with a bright smile.

"I'm good how are you?" The girl replied.

"Oh, I've been better. It's been a day." Nari sighed. "And of course, to top it off, I forget my room key. I don't even feel like bothering my boyfriend is there any way I can get an extra key?"

"I can definitely help you out, but as part of our safety precautions I will have to have you verify some information with you."

"Of course." Nari smiled.

Because she was able to confirm his first and last name, address, and the last 4 numbers of the card on file Nari had a key in a matter of minutes.

As Nari took the room key from the lady she glanced down at her wrist where she got his name tattooed, he had hers too. On his chest. Impulsive, bad decisions made by the pair when they were 18. Her eyes watered, as each step became heavier.

"Oh, that tattoo is not going to age well if he is cheating," Camile leaned in to tell her. "Skully got a mean coverup game though."

If looks could kill, Camile would be dead right there in the hotel lobby. "Ima go back to being quiet."

When they made it up to the room, Nari stood outside of the door for a minute. Each of the ladies stood beside her patiently waiting.

Nari's stomach was in knots.

There was no turning back now.

She slipped the key in the door and led the way inside the hotel.

The evidence of another woman was all over the room.

From the purple duffle bag in the corner of the room, to the Tory Burch purse that sat on the bedside table.

Nari licked her lips, nodding her head. Neither of them was in sight, but it was obvious by the sound of running water from the bathroom what was going on.

"Nari, we can just leave baby girl." Camile rubbed her back gently.

"No. I'm good, I'm so good. But this hotel room ain't." She laughed crazily.

Before either of them could wonder where she was going with that, she knocked the tv off the table. Followed by the lamp. Then it was just everything in sight.

"Oh, I'll get her clothes." Storm squealed, going for the duffle bag dumping all its contents onto the bed, and began assisting Nari with making a mess of the place.

When the bathroom door swung open, Torrian was first to step out with a towel wrapped around his face, and the guiltiest expression on his face when his eyes met Nari's.

The girl crept up behind him, eyes wide in fear.

"Nari..."

"Nope." She held her hand up to him. "I know about

her, and the close friends, your little secret messages." Nari calmly took off her jacket, removing her earrings and sliding them safely into her purse.

She started to remove her rings, but stopped herself with a chuckle. "I might actually put these to good use."

"Baby. Can we- can we talk about this?"

"Talk about what Torrian? You're caught! Red-handed! I don't want to talk. I want to fight." She squared up on the spot.

"Baby, she's not even worth you fighting…"

"HER?!?" Nari laughed wildly. "Bitch, I'm about to fuck you up!" She yelled before she walked up and hit him right in the jaw.

Neither Storm nor Camile could decide if they wanted to intervene.

On one accord they knew this situation was getting out of hand. On another, they both imagined themselves in her position.

Not only finding out your man was cheating but catching them in the act.

Nari was angry, humiliated, and hurt. He was going to feel her.

Even as her vision blurred with tears, and he had wrapped his arms around her, holding her tight against him to keep her from striking him.

"Get off of me!" She cried. "Let me go!"

"Let her go." Storm stepped in. "Let her go Torrian!"

"She got to talk to me Storm." He pleaded with his eyes. "I don't care about this hotel, I don't care that you put your hands on me, I don't even care about her... we got to talk about this baby."

What else could he really say?

He was caught red-handed. All he could really do now is fight for his relationship. If there was anything to talk about it.

"We're done Torrian!" Nari yelled still trying to wiggle out of his tight hold.

There's nothing to talk about."

"Then I'm not letting go, because I can't let you go." His voice went weak.

"I'm not playing with you Torrian, let me go!"

"Torrian let her go!" Storm shouted. "And bitch would you go put some clothes on!" She yelled at the girl still standing there in her towel. "Get the hell out. Do something other than stand there looking stupid as hell, because you look like you want to get your ass beat."

The girl had some sense. Enough to know that she was outnumbered and had better choose her actions wisely. Just not enough to know not to mess with someone else's man.

"No! She can stay. She can really stay. I hope she got a house you can sleep at while you sneak around in hotels! I hope she got a car you can use! Nigga got my whole name tattooed on his chest and got the nerve to be... ohh let me go!"

Torrian refused.

At some point Nari stopped fighting, she had

exhausted herself. Nari's angry tears turned to her full out bawling from the hurt.

While Torrian just held her close refusing to let go. He wasn't even pleading his case anymore. He was just holding her close while the opportunity was still there.

———

Eventually Storm had called Brennon.

Unfortunately, security had arrived before he did.

Neither Nari nor Torrian said much when the police arrived, Torrian took responsibility for the damages and was slapped with an expensive fee and a ban from the hotel for three years.

By the time everyone made it home, it was after 2 in the morning. Brennon had dropped Camile off and Torrian was crashing on the couch for the night.

"Don't tell me you're mad at me too."

Brennon had entered the room after he'd just had a talking to with his brother. Storm could tell he was pissed still.

"Why would you even be a part of some goofy shit like that Storm?" He questioned. "You had the opportunity to defuse that whole situation before it even started. You could have warned me."

"For what? So, you could give Torrian's punk ass a heads up!" Storm frowned. "Did you know he was cheating on that girl?"

"No, and to be frank I don't really give a damn

because it's none of my business." Brennon answered. "Just like it's none of yours."

"Nari is my friend."

"And?!?"

"And I was going to be there for her when she needed me. Even if it meant exposing your cheating ass, brother. So yes, I could have interfered, but no, I didn't because Torrian deserves everything he got and then some. You don't seem to think. I'm not concerned about your brother being butt hurt about it, but what does concern me is you seem to not have a problem with what he's done."

"I'm not proud of the shit, and we gon have that discussion and I'll hold him accountable. But come on he's a 20-year-old kid."

"He's not a kid! We were together at 20, did you give yourself a hall pass then too?"

"No, but we also took a break after high school. Why? Because we were too young, trying to move too fast, and neither of us were ready. They're in over their heads is all I'm saying. What 20-year-old boy you know is trying to settle down?"

Storm rolled her eyes. "There's a right and wrong way to do everything. If you're not ready to be faithful in a relationship, you don't have to be in one, but you have to say that! You don't get to have your cake and eat it too!"

Brennon let out a heavy sigh. "This isn't even our

argument to have." He shook his head. "That's their drama. My only point is stay out of it!"

"Thank you again for this opportunity Lee." Skully smiled in amazement. They had arrived at the convention roughly an hour and a half to get ready.

"Stop thanking me." Lee brushed her off. "You earned this shit. We bout to get this money." He ran his hands together eagerly.

"Really, it means a lot to me. I hold you in such high regard. When I see you on your business shit, the way you hold it down. I don't know how you do what you do."

"You don't? You don't think you'll be in my same position one day, with your own shop?"

"You think I could? You wouldn't feel any type of way?"

"Skully, some people are just meant to be bosses. I know what dope, talent I have in my shop. And I know which of my employees are going to remain just that. They're content, they're making their money, and they don't have any interest beyond that because they're more than happy to not have my type of stress."

"But just because I think I'm a boss, does that really mean I'm ready to be one? I mean the more I sit back and soak up knowledge from you the more I don't think I am."

"I'm telling you you're your own worst enemy girl. We all are." Lee shook his head. "You don't get to be a leader without being a good follower. Luckily, you got one of the best to look up to. When you're ready to take off the training wheels you'll know. Until then, I'm here for whatever you need."

"Preciate ya. Well…. You know my flight heads out tonight."

"Yeah, I saw. You sure you want to dip out early? Now that the hard works done, you deserve a lil fun."

"I got some things to handle back home."

"Oh yeah? Back home." Lee replied. "You still staying with Law?"

"I am. That really doesn't seem to sit right with you."

"It's not that. I just see two good people that I care about- that I don't know are good for each other."

Lee could see her considering his words, as he continued. "I'm just trying to look out. You've both experienced years of a toxic relationship, toxic in different ways, but the toxicity is there."

"You think I'm too toxic for your cousin?" She placed a hand on her hip.

"Not at all, but y'all could be toxic for each other if y'all hop into something before you're ready. I think you're both equally capable of hurting each other, without even trying."

"Lee you've been having my back, coming in the clutch for a lil minute now. I appreciate you for it.

This is just one of those things I got to see for myself."

"How was the gym last night?" Wilma smirked.

Camile looked from her mother-in-law to her fiancé. She took a big bite of her egg, bacon, and cheese bagel.

"Good!" She answered. "I'm seeing the results."

"I'm not." Wilma stated.

Wilma had been staying with them 2 weeks now and Camile couldn't wait for her home renovations to be finished so she could go back home.

Camile gawked looking over at Jeremiah waiting for him to say something to his mother.

"I told you to cut it with all that gym nonsense. Your body is perfect to me, but ima support you in whatever you do." He leaned in to whisper in her ear. "With ya fine ass."

"Um, huh. You just want some cooch." She giggled back.

"I do, I do, I dooo…" he sang.

Camile looked up to see Wilma frowning over at her from across the kitchen, she stuffed her mouth full of bagel again to mask her laughter.

"Well, I heard you weren't at the gym. I heard you were up at that hotel cutting up like you in high school still." Wilma accused.

Camile rolled her eyes to the ceiling. Somehow, someway, Wilma always knew everything.

She hadn't told Jeremiah about the incident yet, and she was certain he hadn't talked to the other men.

"What is she talking about?" Jeremiah questioned.

"It's a long story. I'll fill you in later. You might want to call Torrian though. Nari caught him cheating and beat his ass last night." Camile snickered.

"What?!?" Jeremiah was shocked. "How the hell I always miss everything?"

"It's better that way son. You don't need to be out here showing your ass like these heffas and hooligans." Wilma stated shaking her head.

Camile just let that ride, sometimes you just didn't dignify Wilma's slick comments with a response.

"So, that boy was really out here and none of us knew?" Camile concluded shaking her head. She could tell by Jeremiah's reaction he had been just as in the dark.

11

*J*effery and Kimba in the same space, you never knew what you were going to get.

In most instances Law's parents could be cordial, which was tremendous growth. Still, there were times they still bickered back and forth like an old married couple.

"If we didn't do anything else right, we created some beautiful, brilliant kids," Jeffery stated.

"They get that from me." Kimba boasted.

"Yeah, I'll let you have that. Like I was saying..." he continued. "As a parent, we tend to want more for our kids than what we had. We didn't get it all right, but it brings me much joy and pride to say you meet and surpass all my expectations of you. Congratulations son."

"Preciate you old man." They shared a hug.

"I just want to say how proud I am of you, Bro.

You've come such a long way and did some amazing things in a short period of time so I can't wait to see you continue to grow. Congratulations Law school!" Terrance exclaimed.

"Thank you." They dapped each other up.

Sharing this big moment with his peers, mentor, and most important to him- his family meant the world to him.

As happy as he was, there had been a dark cloud following him all day. The void of who was missing.

In his head he saw his sister's beautiful smiling face. He could hear her soothing voice and kind words on repeat because Amira always knew just the thing to say.

Amira had a way about her that made dark days feel lighter, and the air feels fresher. Her absence was felt, her presence was missed.

"Well, you already know how I feel about you." Kimba started fanning her eyes as though the tears were already on the way. "About how proud you've made me..." her voice cracked. "Against all odds you've prevailed, and never for a second did I not think you would accomplish great things..."

"Not even a second?" Terrance teased.

"Shut up boy." Kimba chuckled. "Congratulations! I love you."

Law walked around to hug and kiss his mother on the cheek. "Love you too mama."

"I hope I'm not interrupting..." Tatum approached them.

"You always are," Terrance muttered.

"Terrance." His mother nudged him.

Tatum made her rounds, greeting everyone, except Terrance.

Tatum looked stunning. Her luscious fro, glowing skin, and beautiful smile were the perfect combo. She wore a black, one shoulder jumpsuit. With a pair of pearl embellished at the vamp and ankle cuff, Jimmy Choo opened toed heels, and a matching pearl clutch.

"You look handsome." They shared a tight hug.

"Thank you." He pulled away, looking her in the face. "Congratulations, gorgeous."

"Thank you." Tatum breathed a sigh of relief. "We started this thing together and now here we are."

"We did."

Law knew there was a conversation that needed to be had. They were close to crossing a line again, but with them there were never really any lines.

However, there was a time and place for everything and now was not the time to talk about something like this.

"Now this is the final award of the night," Mr. Dixon announced. "Most improved. I couldn't think of a more fitting person. When I met this person, I instantly saw the potential, but they were rough around the edges. It took me all of 3 minutes of meeting this person to know why they chose law school, because they had a rebuttal for everything."

There was a brief pause for the laughter that followed the comment.

"It quickly became a pleasure to not only be a part of but watch this person's growth. I could go on, but I'll just leave it at this. Congratulations. I know you'll take all your knowledge and experience and truly make a difference in this world. Mr. Walker, come on up."

Law was both shocked and honored. Mr. Dixon was held in such high regard in his eyes that this moment couldn't have been any better.

He accepted his award and took a few pictures with Mr. and Mrs. Dixon.

He was heading back to his seat when his breath caught in his throat. His whole demeanor changed as he headed toward the entrance instead.

Tatum's head turned and her nose immediately turned up.

He watched as Skully smoothed her dress over as he approached.

"Hi Lawrence." She greeted him with a quick smile.

"Hi." Law replied taking her in.

Under his scrutiny Skully felt herself getting a little anxious.

Dresses weren't her everyday attire, but it wasn't like she didn't know she was a baddie.

Skully wore a chocolate satin drape blazer dress, with a pair of gold- pointed toe heels that she tied around her ankle. Her hair was in a long, sleek, braided weave ponytail.

Her face was bare, but she'd managed to glue on some lashes and the cutest brown lippie.

"You look…" he stopped and made the chef's kiss gesture. "I didn't think you were going to come."

"You weren't holding your breath or anything. You weren't thinking about little ole me."

"You don't even know how untrue that is." He took her by the hand. "Let me introduce you to my folks." He led the way to the table.

Skully had never had the nerves that came with meeting the parents or having to make a good impression on them.

Her ex was a piece of shit, raised by pieces of shit. What did it matter? What they had or hadn't thought of her?

With Law's parents they would either accept her or they wouldn't.

"Everyone, this is Skully." Law introduced. "Skully, this is my mother Kimba, father Jefferey, and my brother Terrance…" As he went around the table he came to a natural pause at Tatum. She was present therefore she deserved an introduction, but it felt awkward.

In ways it felt like the clash of his past and his future.

He and Tatum had history, and memories- good and bad. There was a lot between them.

On the other hand, there was Skully. She was just unapologetically Skully in every way and he loved everything about that.

"...Skully, this is Tatum. My ex-girlfriend."

"We've met." Skully nodded her head. "It's nice to meet all of you." Skully smiled as Law pulled out a chair for himself.

"Law didn't mention he was bringing a date." Kimba stated. It didn't sound as though she meant anything by it. She just genuinely seemed surprised and one of the most inviting smiles. "I just have to say, my son hasn't even mentioned you but I'm not even surprised. That's my son for you."

"Well, he mentioned her to me." Jefferey teased. It brought him a little satisfaction, like he had one up in the childish competition between the parents.

"Well, we all know Law is a mama's boy." Tatum quipped. "So, if he didn't tell mama, we all know what that means."

Terrance couldn't stand the smug expression. "Well, I've heard plenty about you and Law doesn't bring just anybody around, so if you're meeting ma that's saying something."

Skully flashed Terrance a quick smile. Not that she needed anyone to have her back, but it was appreciated.

"He didn't know I was going to make it. I didn't

even know if I would." Skully explained. "I was away at a conference for work."

"Hm. What do you do?" Kimba seemed more interested than nosy.

"I'm a tattoo artist."

"You did the tattoo of my baby girl, didn't you?"

"Yes ma'am."

"Beautiful job by the way." Kimba complimented her.

"Thank you!" Skully smiled.

"I know he has a whole slew of them, but that one really means a lot to him, you know. Amira... she meant a lot to all of us."

"I'm sure. If I can offer anything to you all it's that she lives on through you. As long as you're alive, celebrating her life and keeping her memories alive, she lives on through you. I have to constantly remind myself about my father."

"Sorry for your loss and thank you for those very kind words." Kimba apologized.

"I can't thank y'all enough for being here. Y'all know how much harder it was to have that same motivation after Amira died... the way she did." Law cleared his throat. "Each of you have played your vital roles leading up to this moment." He squeezed Skully's hand a little tighter. "I love y'all for that man."

Skully flashed her a genuine smile, "Well, I didn't want to be rude and not at least come speak first, but I saw food and I'm pretty excited about it! If y'all would excuse me…"

"I'll get it for you."

"Nonsense."

"You might want to take me up on my offer. You're barely making it in those heels." He teased.

Skully couldn't hold back her loud laugh. She could take a joke. "Lawrence, sit down!"

Tatum felt sick to her stomach witnessing them all smiley and giddy in her face. "Oh, he hates when people call him that."

"Not me." Skully grinned before turning away. "I'll be back."

"Nari!!! Open the damn door!" Torrian shouted in frustration. He'd been at it for over 40 minutes.

Nari's music was turned up as loud as it could go, she could drown him out all night.

As stubborn as she was, there was a part of her that wondered what he had the balls to say.

"I know you're here!"

"What gave it away?" She opened the door, meanwhile the screen-door remained locked. "My car in the driveway." She said sarcastically.

On the outside Nari looked pulled together, with her hair in a French braid down her back, a red-cropped hoodie, and a pair of black leggings.

Her intrapersonal, on the other hand, was all fucked up. Just the night before she'd cried what she deemed her "last tears".

Which was how she was able to stand before him, with the barrier of a screen door between them, with a straight face.

"You changed the locks?" Torrian questioned. "I don't even have a key to my own house. You really on your cut up shit, huh?"

Everything they had- they'd pretty much got together. Something that she had taken pride in prior to all of this.

All through senior year of high school, they stacked up and moved out together post-graduation. He covered rent. They went half on LG&E and she paid the water bill. They'd bought a used car that he paid the high ass insurance for. Everything was a collaborative effort.

Nari wasn't sure if she was ready to handle everything on her own, but what other choice did she have?

Nari let out a heavy sigh, "Boy, what do you want?" She crossed her arms.

"To talk. For you to hear me out. To get some clothes."

"You want to talk, or you want some clothes?"

"Both. Baby, I just want to be around you in whatever capacity that has to be. Whether you're cussing me out the whole time or beating my ass. I just need to at least know you're going to give me that chance. So, we can get back."

"What makes you think I'm giving you another chance? I don't need you to explain anything."

"Look, I know you're hurting and all that right now. Once you let go of that stubborn pride, you know what it is with us. Don't sit here and act like it's that easy to throw away." There came the cockiness. "Eventually we gon have to be adults about this. We gon have to talk."

"You don't get to tell me about my hurt and you damn sure don't have the right to talk to me about being an adult when you can't even be a man and give me the same loyalty, I've given you for 4 years!"

People could call it puppy love all they wanted, Nari was all in.

There wasn't anything anyone could tell her about Torrian.

"The thing that hurts the most..." She shook her head. "I don't even think you realize how bad you've hurt me, and I don't really think you're sorry for anything other than getting caught. You think you're going to smooth talk your way out of this or sex me back into stupidity but you're not sir. And this isn't my pride or my ego. This is me trading in my rose-tinted glasses, for my niggas ain't shit lenses. *I can see clearly now.* You've shown me who you are. I received it and I believe it."

Nari had nothing more to say, and no interest in

anything else he had to say- so she closed the door right in his face.

———

"I appreciate you coming tonight. Looking up and seeing your face... I can't even lie, that was like the highlight of my night." Law told her.

They lied next to each other in her bed, staring up at the ceiling. They'd been home for over an hour. Neither of them had even bothered getting out of their clothes. They'd been talking, with Skully's playlist playing in the background.

"You gon just sit up here and make me blush like that?" She smiled. "Is that what you want?"

"I want to make you blush, I want to make you smile, I want to make you happy, and I want to make this official."

"Whew." She exhaled. "That's a lot of dip on your chip."

"I can do it all if you'll let me. I know I got to prove myself and earn your trust. I'll do that, whatever it takes. I just want to be with you."

He took the air out of her with that sentiment.

It had been so long since she'd felt anything, much less this level of affection. It's the sort of thing she would typically run and hide from.

"You know what else I want to do, like right now?"

"Right now?" She arched her eyebrow.

"Right now." He confirmed.

"Oh. I'm curious now."

"I want to make you cum."

Her mouth fell wide open. "Lawrence!"

"It's this freaky ass playlist."

Skully laughed. "You love my playlists."

"I love you." He confessed. It had just rolled right off his tongue before he could even catch himself.

He didn't want to catch himself. He just wanted to keep it real with her, even if that was scary for him.

Skully shot up, looking over at him. For a long time, they just stared back at one another.

"I want to show you something..." She told him. Standing up before him.

His eyes didn't leave her body as she peeled the dress off. He swallowed the lump in his throat as he sat up.

They'd had sex, but this was his first time seeing her body in full display.

It was an added layer of intimacy. As she took his hand and trailed it along the scaring across her stomach.

"He tried to kill me," she started to explain after a minute. "He didn't succeed, but I have a daily reminder every single time I look at my body." Her eyes fluttered to the ceiling as she refused the tears that threatened to fall. "I could've easily covered it with tattoos. The thought has crossed my mind plenty, but I- I didn't want to hide it, that's what I do with everything. I hide my pain, I hide my feelings, and I hide behind this wall I've built around myself because I just don't want to get hurt again. But I don't want to hide anymore, and I don't think you would hurt me."

"I won't."

"Okay."

She didn't know whether she believed him. She just knew that she would want to.

She lied back on the bed, now stripped down to her bra and thong.

He hovered over her and began placing gentle kisses from her neck to her breast. He freed her titties from her bra and showed them both love before making his way down her belly to her scar.

He kissed every part of her, like his kisses were the remedy to make it disappear. He kissed her whole body like he could free it of all its pain.

Then he made his way back to the creases of her thighs. He pulled her body to the very edge of the bed and got down on his knees.

By the time he blessed her pussy with the slow, long swirls of his tongue Skully was squirming.

He was making her body feel good, and her heart feel full.

He had said he loved her and if he hadn't proved it with his words, he was going to do so with his tongue.

Law sucked and slurped until she came and then licked her clean after.

She was panting like she'd just ran a marathon

when he stood over her positioning himself between her legs.

She wrapped her legs around his waist, using her thighs to pull him close.

His mouth fell open as he relished in how good she felt.

"Lawrence..." He paused still deep inside of her as he looked right into her eyes. "You make me feel so good. I appreciate that. I appreciate you." Her eyes were misty, as he looked into them, he understood everything she wasn't saying.

He nodded his head, returning to his rhythmic strokes. "I love you." He poured his heart out to her as he came inside of her.

He didn't love her any less because she didn't say it back. He appreciated her for wanting to try for him, when he knew it was hard for her.

12

"*J*ma let her cool off, but Nari crazy as hell if she thinks she just gon put me out my own house." Torrian shook his head.

"Yeah, okay." Jeremiah shook his head. "You still don't get it brotha. You have opened the floodgates of hell."

"And I still don't get why." Brennon agreed. "I mean, you love the girl?"

"Come on now. I love the hell out of the girl, how could you even question that?"

"Because that's what happens when you cheat. Even if she were to take you back, she's going to spend every minute after that questioning that same thing."

Torrian let out a heavy sigh. Actions always had consequences he hadn't weighed before he jumped off the deep end.

"Crazy thing is I don't even see it for ole girl like

that. I was about to dead it with her, then here come Nari busting up in that hotel room."

"Oh yeah, and I guess it's her fault for catching you cheating?" His brother shook his head. "Yeah, you real fucked up."

"Who ain't? I ain't never claimed to be perfect! I got caught up, but you gotta understand where I'm coming from. We were starting to argue all the time and Nari can never just drop it. She's never going to just let shit go..."

"Neither are you."

"What am I supposed to do? Simp out like you? Storm talks to you 10 types of crazy and you let her..."

"Man, I've been happily married for 5-going on 6 years... I could give a fuck about winning a petty argument. So, if I got to bite my tongue sometimes ima do that because I know what I got at home isn't worth losing."

"If holding Storm accountable for her bullshit causes y'all to lose everything y'all have built over 11 years then maybe y'all got more problems than you care to admit. I mean sometimes I don't even know if she even respects you as a man."

Torrian was stepping into dangerous territory.

Not only talking about Brennon's wife, but bringing his manhood into question. Brennon could've knocked him on his back right then and there.

"You out here disrespecting and humiliating your woman, and you think she respects you as a man?"

Brennon chuckled. "You always did have to learn the hard way Torrian, and you still got a lot to learn."

Jeremiah didn't want to get anywhere in between his cousin's back and forth. Especially when they both had a point.

"I'm a lil busy Tatum." Law stated.

"Dang, and you can't even make a little time for me." Tatum replied. "Thought we were better than that."

"That's just what it is right now Tatum." Law told her matter of fact.

He wasn't trying to be harsh or hurt her feelings, it's just what it was. They had gone without having boundaries for so long that Tatum didn't know how to not cross the line. For that reason, he just had to be straight to the point with her.

"Ima have to let you go." He told her. "Later."

Skully had walked in on the latter of the conversation, she could mind her business and tend to put

ting away the groceries all she wanted but the minute she saw Tatum on the screen of Law's cell phone it rubbed her the wrong way.

"I got this chicken tikka masala recipe for dinner. I'm excited about it." Skully announced.

"I will be too." Law replied. "Long as you get it right." He smirked, suppressing his laughter.

It wasn't that Skully couldn't cook, in fact there

were many things that she cooked well. However, she always tried to go outside the lines and try something different and that's always where she always dropped the ball.

"Just for that starve."

He'd already gotten out of his seat to come embrace her. He hugged her from behind.

Storm exhaled, relishing in how good he smelled.

"How was your day?" He asked.

"A mess. Not the work, but the personal… whole lot of unnecessary drama going on in the family and I'm just making a habit of staying out of it."

"It be like that." He still held onto her.

"Speaking of drama, you know that's going to be a problem for me. With your ex. I know y'all got history and I can't dictate who you have in your life. That's not even something I would do, but I just get this sense that she's not going to have the decency to respect what we got going and I'm not with that. Can't have you out here fighting cases, meanwhile I'm catching them."

He chuckled. "I don't want you to think that's going to be a problem for us, because I don't want know problems with you. I'll eliminate all things before it even comes to that."

"You would kill her, for me? I feel so honored Law."

He nearly choked on absolutely nothing.

"I appreciate you saying that honestly. Just keep ole girl in check, so I don't have to."

"Hey girl." Kaice stuck her head in the door.

"Oh, hey!" Storm looked up at her friend. "Did you come over to see little ole me?"

"Umm... not exactly." Kaice answered. "I'm just speaking in passing."

"Wow..." Storm stood up from the bed and they walked downstairs to the common area where everyone was. "I never get invited to y'all lil outings. I'm starting to feel offended."

"You'll be aight." Torrian dismissed her. "Kaice, you ready to roll?"

Storm crossed her arms. "Wait, what if I really did want to go, though?"

"It wouldn't matter, because nobody invited you." Torrian reminded her.

"Babe..." Storm pouted.

"Storm, if you really want to come, get dressed."

Storm didn't even enjoy parties, but for the sake of avoiding conflict he would just extend the invite.

"Well, when you say it like that, I wouldn't even want to come. Like, do you even want me to come?"

"I'm just trying to have a good time, so come on, girl. Go get dressed."

"Aight ima stay home." Torrian stated.

"Damn, why it gotta be all that? If it's a boy's night it's a boy's night, but Kaice's coming so it's clearly not. So why can't I go?"

"Because you're not Kaice, and we don't want you there."

"Well, I don't want to go, anyway. Have fun." Storm said in the driest tone.

"Aight we out. Love you."

Storm was so used to Brennon going out of his way to bend to her every wish that it actually aggravated her that he'd let it go that easily.

———

Hours later, when woke from her sleep, she used the bathroom and checked in on Jelani like she normally would.

Then prepared to press her husband on his where-abouts until the laughter coming from downstairs caused her to stall.

"What's so funny?" Storm questioned, stepping right in front of the living room TV with her arms crossed.

Something about Kaice and Brennon sitting on the couch had her feeling a type of way. They looked a little too comfortable for her liking.

"It wouldn't even make sense to you." Kaice dismissed. "You had to be there."

"Yeah well, it seems I'm never invited, so..." Storm commented.

Kaice scrunched up her face in confusion, sensing Storm's sour mood. "Storm, are you good?"

"I'll be even better when you leave, and I can have some alone time with my husband."

"Why are you talking like that?"

"You feeling a way about it?"

"I'm just going to head home, because she's trippin." Kaice stood from the couch, grabbing what was left of her Waffle House to clear the living room table.

"Yeah, please do."

"Okay, what's your problem with me?" Kaice's head turned around so quick.

"Maybe if you had a husband, you could understand how frustrating it is to have a husband who will barely spend time with you but has all the time in the world for everyone else. I mean, is there something I should know about?"

"Why don't you just say whatever it is you're really trying to say, Storm!"

"Are you messing with my husband?" She had managed to ask the question with a straight face, despite it not even feeling right coming out of her mouth.

In fact, Storm felt a little out of her body. Where were all these insecurities coming from? This distrust for the people she actually trusted the most.

"Are you really asking me some shit like that right now?" Kaice questioned.

Storm looked over at Brennon who wasn't even offering a response. He sat there blank faced.

She needed something from him, but he was giving nothing. She looked back to Kaice.

"Woww." Kaice shook her head in disbelief. She took a step back. "I don't even know what you been going through here lately, but ima leave while we're ahead because this is going somewhere, we don't need to go."

"You didn't answer the question! Is it really so far-fetched? I mean I have everything you want, a husband and a child."

"So now I want to be you? Is that it?" Kaice chuckled, growing visibly upset. "You're right, if only I could have a husband who barely can even stand to be around me. You're so fucking self-absorbed that you can't even see how intolerable you really are. If you didn't have so many people who actually love you, you'd probably have no one because you get a pass for a lot of shit you do. Oh, that's just Storm." She emphasized. "Or maybe you're a bitch and it's actually a character flaw."

Storm had hit below the belt. In response Kaice hit lower.

"If I'm so damn intolerable, why are you always around? Always smiling in my face, and my husbands for that matter. Having me in your life is the best part of yours. You love to live vicariously through me bitch. Were you ever really a friend or just a fan?"

Anyone else would've got popped for less, but

because it was Storm, Kaice couldn't bring herself to put hands on her.

"When you run this back, and you realize just how fucked up in the head you are and what you just did. Realize that not only was I a damn good friend to you, but I've always been one of your biggest fans and supporters right, wrong or indifferent. And now I'm neither."

Kaice didn't even bother cleaning up the rest of her things before she turned to walk out of the door.

Storm turned back to Brennon. "You're just going to sit there and not say anything?"

More silence.

It was eating her up.

"Say something!" She shouted.

He just looked at her a little longer, before shaking his head and dismissing her and then himself by walking toward the basement. Of course, the man cave.

Storm rushed to get ahead of her. "Brennon, talk to me! Say something! Tell me that I'm crazy! Defend yourself!"

"Hm." He stopped and chuckled looking down at her with a scowl that willed her to look away avoiding eye contact. "It's the fact that I even have to... I can't even fucking look at you right now."

Skully walked into the living room and dropped her bags to the floor, releasing an exhale as she stepped out of her shoes.

"Relaxed, yet?" Law smirked.

"Almost." She walked over to hug him. "Hi Lawrence." She inhaled his scent.

He placed a kiss on her forehead.

When they finally pulled apart, they sat down together on the couch.

"How was your day?" He questioned.

"A day." Skully sighed. "Some 16-year-old got over with a fake ID the other week, so her mother came clocking out in the shop today."

Law laughed. "Yeah, that sounds like a day."

"I'm so ready for this break. I know you got a few weeks before you start your internship after gradua-tion... you got a lil turn up in you?"

"What'd you have in mind?"

"Can't remember if I mentioned it, but I'm in a wedding. My cousins having a destination wedding in Florida. They're renting this big ass Airbnb. It's dope. Everybody's heading out the Thursday before the wedding."

"Yeah. I can fit that in. I think I need a break too."

"Yeah, I think we're going to have a ball. I have to fill you in on all the drama going on through because I just know... there's going to be more to it. Oh yeah and we're driving..." She slid the last part in.

"Driving? To Florida??? That's like a 13-hour."

"Sounds worse than it actually is. We'll split the drive up. We used to drive for all our family trips. I'm a good travel partner."

"I'm just trying to figure out why you'd rather do a 13-hour car ride, instead of a 3-hour flight."

"Because um… I may or may not be deathly afraid of airplanes."

"You? Scared? Come on now, don't tell me that."

"Don't do me like that. You down to ride or not?"

"For you I guess…" he shook his head. "13 damn hours."

13

2-Weeks Later

Skully hated long ceremonies.

However, she loved the ability to be there in support of Law on his big day.

Skully maintained her distance.

Not because his family made her feel anything short of comfortable. Just because they were still new, and while she could enjoy celebrating these moments, she wanted them to be able to have theirs.

"Well don't just stand there taking all the pictures. Get in some!" Kimba insisted.

After all the picture portion of the ceremony, the family waited while Law made his rounds.

"I'll be back," Skully excused himself.

She eventually made it through the crowd to the bathroom.

In the middle of washing her hands, Tatum entered the bathroom.

Her annoyance immediately set in, because Tatum's smirk alone just read- she was on bullshit.

"Well, congratulations Orphan Annie. You got you a scholar." She gave her a mock round of applause.

Skully released an exasperated sigh, "You know... I would be mad too. You miss it. I get it, that really sucks for you. That's all you get to do because I'm going to have him so wrapped around me it'll be- Tatum who?"

With that Skully cut the water off and flicked the water from her wet hands right in Tatum's face.

"Now y'all really got me fucked up!!!" Camile was in rant mode.

"Camile..." Storm interjected.

"No, no, no..." Camile shook her head. "You had your bridezilla moment. A couple of them. Let me have this!"

"Touché." Storm set back.

Whatever lashing she was about to get was probably deserved. It was more than she was getting from her own husband and best friend.

Except for the things they had to discuss, Brennon gave her nothing.

Kaice was paying her dust in general.

"The one time, I just need everyone to keep it

together y'all want to fall apart! Right before my wedding?!? Ima tell y'all like this-" She stopped pointing between both Storm and Torrian. "Everybody who I paid for a plate for will be at that wedding! And you're going to behave, look good for all the pretty pictures, and stand and sit by whoever the hell I put you next to! And no more plus ones! Kaice got a plus one..."

"What?" Storm stopped, shaking her head. "If Kaice was seeing someone I would know because..."

"Oh, I just know you weren't going to say because y'all are friends!!! You have two pre-requisites as a matron of honor; to be a friend and to be a married woman and you 2 for 0."

"Storm earned her spot in the hot seat, but what did I even do? Why am I here? What I do?" Torrian questioned.

"What haven't you done? Your infidelities started the whole rift in the group. Now Nari got the nerve to think she got a plus one... I cannot!"

"Nari's bringing someone to the wedding?"

"Yes. So now I got another mouth to feed! Thank you for that!"

"Are we done here?" Storm asked. "I do have things to do Camile."

"Um huh whatever. My closing point is simple, act like y'all got some damn sense at my wedding and leave the drama at home!"

Brennon stepped into the room, fresh off work.

All he wanted to do was shower and go to bed.

"Jelani…" Storm shook her daughter's shoulder.

"I'm not sleep…" Jelani groaned.

"You've been saying that for the past 30 minutes. Go to bed, kid." Storm stated.

"Why can't I just sleep with you? Daddy's always in his mancave, anyway." Jelani engrossed herself further into the covers.

"That's not true." Storm denied.

"Um huh." Jelani nodded her head. "Uncle said it's because you're nutty as a cake, but I think he was just being silly because cakes don't have nuts in them."

Brennon chuckled. "I think he said nutty as a fruit-cake Nari and he said that because she is, and fruit-cakes do have nuts."

Storm gawked dramatically but wasn't even surprised he paid her no mind.

"That has nothing to do with you going to bed, though. Good night Jelani."

Jelani made a show of "sleep walking" out of the room.

"Are you going to sleep in our bed tonight?" She asked.

"Yeah."

What did that matter? Strom felt more distance

between them when they were together than when they were apart.

"Are we going to talk about everything Brennon?"

"Yeah, we can talk."

Good. That was a step in the right direction.

If she could at least get him talking, and he would stop being so cold with her they could get back on track.

The lingering silence triggered him. "Aight Ima get in the shower."

"Bren!!! You said we were going to talk…"

"Then say something!!! Because if you still sitting here with nothing to say after the shit you pulled… I damn sure don't have anything to say to you, Bruh."

"Bruh? Don't call me that shit! I'm your wife!"

"Then act like it!!"

All he had to do was walk in the room and her whole mood just changed. Her libido just came alive.

"I mean I know I'm wrong, but…" Her sister continued over the phone.

"If you know you're wrong, why is there even a but Strom?" Skully questioned. "Just admit you're wrong and own that shit."

"I can do that, but no one else is owning theirs. Why should I?" Storm retorted. "Like if there's really nothing going on, why not just say that?"

"Oh my Lord!" Skully exclaimed. "Storm! You've created a problem that's not even a problem and for whatever reason you're running with it even though you know you don't even have a leg to stand on with this bullshit. I wouldn't entertain you with a response either, because I don't even understand why you're playing with that man. You know he's not cheating! Now you want *him* to take accountability. Something that you never do, but in a way we're all to blame, really. This is what you always do this is just your first time being called on it."

"Wow. So, you really just taking everyone else's side like that?"

"This is childish Storm, and I just don't have any more time to entertain it."

"Like you have anything better to do."

"Law just came home, so you know what? I do! Good luck, all of this is unfortunate. Especially for Brennon, he's a good man but now he has to deal with the monster he helped create. Girl… if you don't get it together, you're going to blow it."

"Bye Skully. Go blow Law."

Skully cried, laughing as her sister hung up in her ear.

"What y'all over there talking about?" Law turned to her from the other side of the bed.

"Not much. Storm just gave me a really good idea though." Skully grinned.

"Aren't you going to let me in?" Skully questioned from the porch.

A couple nights had passed, and the wedding was inching closer. If she could play any part of bringing everyone back together, she would attempt it, because she needed her sister to have someone to call on other than her.

"No." Was Kaice's short response. "Don't even come over here caping for your sister."

"Come on." Skully tilted her head to the side. "I came over here all on my own."

"It doesn't matter if you're here on her behalf, or your own. Same difference." Kaice declared with a shrug. "I don't have anything to say."

"Look I know we… I know I don't…"

"Like me." Kaice finished for her, with a nod.

"I mean I wouldn't say that."

"You wouldn't?"

"I mean I would, but is that really an insult coming from me? Who do I like?"

"Skully get the hell off my porch."

"Wait!" Skully stopped her. "I know I wasn't there, but I heard, and I really do feel bad. Storm was out of pocket. She did the typical Storm thing of sabotaging everything good in her life, because everything is good in her life. But that's the beauty of you and your friendship to Storm. You've always been an amazing friend.

Better than she has been to you, but she needs that. My sister's not perfect, she has her flaws. At the heart of her we know she's a good person. With dickhead tendencies, and sometimes she just has to pretend that she has it all together for the sake of not falling completely apart."

"She always was the more successful twin, so I'm used to it by now. I've always been the fuck up and I'm reminded of it every time I look at Storm's perfect life."

"Is that all?"

"Yep." Storm started to walk away.

"To be fair…" Kaice called after her. "Storms a lot better at painting this picture, but I think you have it a lot more together than you give yourself credit for. I mean, you've fallen but you've always picked yourself back up. You're smart, ambitious, and hell you got the same face. Stop selling yourself short. You the shit too."

"Aww. That really just touched my heart Kaice. Got me feeling all giddy inside." Skully smiled. "Is this a little… is this a little girl crush energy I'm sensing? No shade at all if it is… I mean I always got this fluid vibe from you."

"Fuck outta here Skully." Kaice laughed it off.

"Okay, okay. On a serious note, I really appreciate it. You really do have a way of lifting everyone's spirits and making the people around you feel good. One day you're going to meet your person and all of that is going to be reciprocated. You're going to find that person that treats you good."

"Alright this is getting weird. Go home." Kaice stated. "For the record we still don't like each other."

"Facts."

Storm had repositioned herself countless times, only to end up looking goofy as hell when Brennon walked into the living room.

In her lavender, cupless lingerie set. It was his favorite color on her. She was pulling out all the stops.

From his favorite meal to his favorite dessert- her of course.

He threw his keys on the table and tossed his jacket in the chair. He'd come back from playing basketball.

He couldn't have looked sexier with his sweaty, caramel skin. Storm would lick every last sweat droplet from his body if it came to it.

"Where's Jelani?" He asked.

"With Torrian." Brennon answered.

"He did that for you?"

"I paid him." She walked up from the couch. "But that doesn't matter..." she slid her hands under his shirt, standing on her tippy toes to kiss him.

"What are you doing right now Storm?"

"I'm trying to make love to my husband." She reached for his shorts.

"Nah." He stepped back shaking his head. "You're trying to manipulate this situation, like a little sex is going to make our problems go away. Like all you gotta do is throw some pussy at me and I'm going to fall right back in line. Cause that's what you're used to right? You thought I was gon fall for the same shit you been throwing at me for 11 years. Get over yourself!!"

His words cut deep Storm felt like he'd sliced her up, as tears formed in her eyes.

"And I know you really thought you were doing something with those lamb chops! You don't even make them right. Shit be hella overcooked. I just hype you up because you're my wife and I like to do that. Meanwhile you tear me down every chance you get when I've never even given you any reason to."

"What do you want me to do Brennon? How do I resolve this when you won't even give me a chance?"

"I don't know what to tell you. It's never been more apparent than it is now that you don't respect me."

"Where are you even getting that from. I have nothing but respect for you."

"Yeah, that sounds good." He kissed his teeth. "We done here Storm? Cause I really just want to get my daughter. Only reason I'm still here right now." He muttered the latter.

Even if it wasn't the full truth, he had to say, Jelani made the situation worth sticking through even if he had wanted to walk away.

It wasn't until he was out of sight that Storm allowed herself to bawl into her hands.

"I just really need this man out of my head." Nari sighed. "I need his shit out of this house and there's a part of me that even needs to understand why he did the shit. Like, I know I'm not perfect but what am I missing?"

"Nothing." Her friend Destiny assured her. "What I'm not going to do is let you blame you. We all have imperfections, if he couldn't handle yours, he should've just said that, but you didn't deserve that. No one does. Not after how loyal you've been to him."

Nari nodded her head, "Thank you." A moment of silence passed as Nari repositioned herself on the couch looking over at her friend. Her friend of many years. Many memories. With so much trust between them.

"What about you? As loyal as I've been to you, do I have that in you?"

Destiny stalled. "Of course."

"Then why couldn't you just keep it a buck with me?"

"What are you talking about Nari?"

Nari chuckled bitterly. "You going on this full-on investigation with me to uncover what you already knew. Whole time everything's going on right under my nose. Him telling me I shouldn't be kicking it with y'all. Y'all telling me I shouldn't trust him. Turns out y'all was both right about each other."

Destiny let out a heavy sigh. "I'm sorry." She confessed. "I was torn. I could tell you and have you and her mad at me or I could sit back and mind my business and have you find out who he was for yourself."

"What about me says that I would ever fall out with you for telling me the truth?"

"Everything if it's not what you wanted to be true! Nari there was nothing any of us could ever tell you about that boy. That's a fact!"

Maybe it was a tough pill to swallow, but maybe it was also the truth.

She would've needed proof; she would've needed to see it with her own two eyes. She would've had to learn the hard way, the exact way she did.

Because she wouldn't have wanted to hear it, she would've wanted to kill the messenger, being Destiny.

Finding out on her own and seeing for herself the sneaky shit he was doing behind her back was a necessary evil. Knowing he'd been consistently lying in her face. By the time she walked into that hotel room her image of him was already tainted.

"And who is she to you? What the fuck did you owe her?" Nari questioned.

"She's my cousin, on my daddy's side." Destiny explained.

That blew Nari away. The distance he tried to keep between her, and Destiny made so much more sense now. He worked harder to cover his tracks, then to not hurt her by just falling back altogether.

Nari swallowed the lump in her throat. She was livid. "Get out!"

"What?"

"Destiny, get the fuck out of my house!" Nari hissed. "Get out!!!"

14

*S*torm hated airports from the people, the tedious process, to the hustle and bustle of it all.

She'd had an exhausting night. After work it took hours packing for herself, Brennon, and Jelani. She skipped dinner just to shower and get to sleep sooner. However, she'd just tossed and turned the night away. Leaving her hungry and sleep deprived.

Now that they had made it through the check-in process, Storm had gotten Starbucks and food from Aunt Annie's.

"There goes my appetite." Storm pushed the pretzel dogs away. She'd only eaten a couple, but she couldn't stomach anymore.

When he looked up and saw his brother headed their way, he didn't even have to wonder what she was speaking of. "Fuck is wrong with him?" Brennon said to himself, shaking his head.

Him not riding with them to the airport made much more sense.

"Hey y'all!" He greeted them like all was good with the world.

"Hey!!!" Jelani was the only one to respond. "Who's she?"

Torrian chuckled. "This is Ariel. Ariel, that's my niece Jelani, my brother Brennon and his wife Storm."

"Ariel, like the little mermaid?" Jelani asked.

"Yeah cutie." Ariel smiled. "Like the mermaid. Is it okay if I sit next to you?" She referred to the empty seat to the left of Jelani.

"No." Storm stated blankly.

"Mama…"

"Jelani, eat them pretzels and stop talking to strangers, please. Brennon, get them out of my face."

"Look, I don't want there to be any problems…" Ariel started.

"Let me stop you right there." Storm held up her finger. "You are the problem! Your presence alone on this trip is a problem. This a family wedding and you brought your weird ass here. Girl, you know what you're doing, fuck outta here. Get her out my face because I'm really on that today."

"Control your wife bruh." Torrian kissed his teeth. "Which you never do! Tell her to watch her mouth!"

"Only thing I'm watching is your dog ass moving

hella funny, because you in your feelings because Nari won't take you back."

"I'm moving like a grown ass man who can do what the fuck he wants. It ain't none of your business, but you have a hard time minding that. That's why your marriage is falling apart now. You can call everyone else out, you know everybody else's problems but your own!"

"I don't have a problem!" Storm stood up to put herself at his level.

"You are the problem!!" Torrian barked.

They had already gained the attention of the people around them.

"Aye." Brennon got in between them both. "Both of y'all disrespecting my daughter right now, she doesn't need to be hearing any of this."

"She's always starting something bruh…"

"Oh, I'm not even started yet…"

"Shut the fuck up!!!" Brennon boasted.

Storm bit the hell out of her tongue, taking heed to the warning in her husband's eyes as she returned over to her seat apologizing to Jelani for the commotion.

Brennon strong armed his resistant brother to the side, putting some distance between the two.

"Bruh, you disrespecting the hell out of my wife right now, all of that was unnecessary to say and if we weren't in this airport right now, I would fuck you up right now!" Brennon stated calmly.

Calmly but Torrian knew not to challenge him on that.

Brennon was one of those people that was always so calm, that to see him angry was scary at times.

"You already knew this was going to be a problem, but that's what you wanted. Take that goofy shit on and keep her goofy ass away from my wife, because you already knew this wasn't gon fly."

Torrian brushed past his brother, Brennon could give him the benefit of the doubt of only being 20 but this was just inexcusable for him.

"I'm not dealing with that all weekend." Brennon returned to the table.

"He just…" Storm attempted to come to her own defense.

"I'm not dealing with that." Brennon repeated. "Stay out of it, I'm not saying it again. End of discussion."

"Aht-aht-aht… Stop right there." Camile demanded before they could even get in the door. "It's shot o' clock baby!"

Camile and Jeremiah had left a day ahead of everyone to check in and make sure everything was in order before everyone else arrived.

"I'm not in the mood right now." Skully brushed her off.

"What's wrong with you?" Camile questioned.

"Dude really chose to argue with me the whole last half of the ride."

"Oh Lord, not y'all too. What were y'all into it about?"

"My driving." Law had driven the first half of the ride and Skully had taken over after that.

Skully wasn't here for planes, and while everyone else opted to go the plane route she was grateful Law had been willing to take that 12-hour ride with her.

However, the complaining was nerve wracking.

"Well bitch you were wrong then." Camile stated.

"What?"

By that point Law was behind them carrying in their bags.

"Law, I feel for you. I've been in the car with her a few times. Sis has gotten away with attempted murder many times. You need this shot. Tilt your head back."

The turn up had officially begun.

As everyone else rolled in, Camile had plenty of drinks, food, and conversation flowing.

"Shot o' clock!" Camile sprung up.

"Nope-no-no." Skully shook her head. "If I drink any more, I'm not going to be any good for the rest of the night."

"Knock, knock…" the door opened, and Brennon entered with arms and hands full of luggage.

Jeremiah walked over to help him. Camile immediately went into host mode. "Shot o'clock!"

"No ma'am, no ma'am." Storm shook her head. "Then again, double it I probably need that liquor."

"Not you too." Camile rolled her eyes. "What's the problem?"

Before Storm could answer Torrian came walking in, "I know y'all didn't get the party started without me."

"Hi, everyone." Ariel walked into the house offering a polite smile. "I'm..."

"The problem, got it." Camile nodded her head downing the shot she had offered Storm.

Skully looked over at Law, who was filled in on all the juicy details. "Told ya. Drama."

"Everyone, this is Ariel." Torrian introduced, then proceeded to go around the room introducing her to everyone individually.

"Torrian let me talk to you for a second." Camile stated.

"I was about to get into some of this good food." Torrian rubbed his hands together.

"Oh, I must've said it like it was optional." Camile chuckled. "Bring your dirty ass over here." She pulled him into the other room. "What the hell are you going through? Why would you bring her here?"

"So, it's okay for Nari to have a plus one but I can't?" He challenged.

"Unless she's rolling up in here with a nigga, she cheated on you with, it's not the same thing!"

"Well, y'all don't get to dictate who I deal with. Neither does Nari."

"Wow... I can't even believe you right now."

"It's whatever." Torrian shrugged. "Ima be the bad guy in your eyes anyway, because you're on her side."

"Would you grow the hell up? It's not about a side! You hurt that girl, stabbed her right in the back, and now you're just twisting it. She won't be here until the rehearsal dinner. You still have a chance. Get that girl out of here Torrian."

Torrian considered it for a minute.

It made perfect sense. It hurt to hear that Nari was bringing a date, but when he'd hurt her so badly to begin with, did he even have a right to be hurt?

"Nah." Torrian shook his head returning to the other room.

"Well, I don't know what she gon eat. That hoe is not accounted for." Camile muttered, "I done told y'all about all these plus ones." She placed her hands on her hips.

They'd already called to warn Nari, but the truth is she'd distanced herself from all the girls and Camile wasn't even so sure she was still coming.

They were going to make a mess of her wedding; she was sure of it.

"Where's the closest bathroom?" Ariel asked.

"...Down that hall to the right." Jeremiah answered.

There was a silent pause when she walked out of the room.

"You wild." Jeremiah pointed. "If I knew that's who you were bringing, I would've never given you the green light. Ima get blamed for this."

"You damn right." Camile smacked him playfully in the back of his head. "I said no more plus ones." She stressed.

"I just don't understand why somebody's so invested in who I'm with." Torrian stated.

"You understand." Camile rolled her eyes. "Storm, I'm surprised you being so calm."

Storm had a mouth full she wanted to say but stalled when she looked over at Brennon. "My husband told me to shut the hell up so that's what I'm gon do." She made the motion to zip her lips. "My name is Bennett and I ain't in it."

"Let me go check on my sister," Skully stood.

"She might've dodged a lot of shops with her little nap, but she's not dodging these balls in her face tonight!" Camile shouted. At that point she was wasted, and the night was only getting started.

The men and the women would be going their separate ways for the night.

Everyone had gotten dressed, and pre-gamed which they had basically been doing the entire day.

"I got it." Brennon insisted.

When he walked inside the bedroom, Storm's back was to him.

"You okay?" He asked taking a seat at the edge of the bed.

"You care?" Storm retorted.

"Storm…"

"How many times do I have to apologize?"

It wasn't enough that he was coming to check on her, because that was just Brennon, his protective nature. Didn't change anything.

"As many times as you need to make you feel better. Those are just words to me." He shrugged.

"What do you want me to do Bren? Beg?" She crawled on her knees to the edge of the bed. She wrapped her arms around him from behind. "I've upset my best friend and my husband. Do you not think this is humiliating enough?"

"I want you to mean it!" He shouted.

"I do!" She yelled back. Stepping off the bed, and onto her feet to look him right in the eyes.

"You don't! You want me to forgive you because it's what you want! Not because you're even taking the time to understand how fucked up it has me that after 11 years that was some shit you could even accuse me of! I'm a man of principle and integrity and you treat me like I'm not shit. Is that the type of man you think I am?!?"

"No." That's all she had to offer.

Even she was having a hard time justifying her own actions.

"Then explain it to me, because a lot of shit I let slide over the years, but you gotta help me out here. I bend over backwards for you, and you walk around like your shit don't stink and I let you. You're my wife. If ima put anybody on a pedestal it's gon be you."

It was true, Brennon was the perfect protector and provider. He often read her mind and knew her needs before she did. If Storm ever dropped the ball, he picked it up and never gave her any fuss about it- just held it down.

"I don't even have leg room when it comes to you." He continued. "I can't even forget your mega millions. I could see you cheat with my own two eyes and I would still go get them checked, because that's just how fucked up I am behind you. Babe... are you okay?" He stopped himself. He had more to get off his chest, but that could take a backseat to making sure his wife was okay.

"You look a little out of it." He told her.

"I feel a little woozy. I just feel a little off."

"Come on, you need to come eat some of this food. I haven't seen you eat once today. Come on." He urged, leading her to the kitchen by her hand.

"Look who's back!" They clapped when Storm entered the room.

"What do you want to eat?" Brennon asked.

"Just give me a little of everything." Storm went

over to the couch, she just needed to be off her feet again. She found a comfortable position on her side, because she couldn't catch her breath on her back and laying on her stomach was a no-no.

"Uh-uh Storm, you can sit over there and fake sick all you want baby girl but you're not getting out of tonight." Camile stated. "Just trying to guilt Brennon into staying back with you, you not slick."

"He don't love me like that. He wouldn't do it, anyway."

"You okay, boo?" Skully leaned over the couch.

Storm nodded her head, "I'm good." She lied.

"So, what we gon do? Barbecue or mildew?" Skully questioned.

The men had already left a little over an hour ago.

"Don't you fucking call me mildew, bitch!" Camile barely lifted her head from the couch before she slouched back down.

Storm was still "not feeling good" and Camile was drunk out of her mind. She was supposed to be closing her eyes for just a minute, that had turned into 40.

When the doorbell rang, Skully went to answer it. "Whew. I've never been happier to see you. Look at what I'm stuck with..." She led the way to the living room.

"What the hell happen?" Kaice had not long ago

arrived. She already knew with her late flight to come ready to party, but from the looks of things, she was the only one.

"Camile has been drinking like a fish. Storm has been crying, sick all day, and I'll be honest I don't really care what we do just as long as we're back when my man gets back." Skully stated.

Kaice walked over to them both. "Up, up, up!!! Let's go! Let's go!" Regardless of the rocky nature of her friendship with Storm, they were there for Camile, and all of that could be put aside for the sake of having a good time.

"I'm up. I'm up." Camile stretched. "I just needed a little shuteye. Storm, get your whack ass up!" She went over to the couch opposite of her to be bothersome to her friend. Drumming her booty, she demanded. "Wake up Storm."

"Leave me alone." Storm groaned. "I'm getting up."

Storm winced as she used the cushions and what little strength she could muster to rise from the couch.

She felt her eyes roll to the back of her head.

No sooner than Storm stood from the couch she hit the floor.

"Storm!!!" Skully gasped in shock rushing to her sister's side. "Storm, stop playing. She's playing." Skully laughed nervously. "Storm!!!" Her voice cracked as shook her frail body. "Call an ambulance! Call Brennon!"

"Whew!!!" Torrian was lit up like a Christmas tree. "It's settled, I'm moving here." He was accompanied by three different girls.

Jeremiah shook his head with a chuckle. "He's not hard to please."

"At all." Brennon chuckled.

"This got to be Heaven because God made all these ass and titties!" Torrian exclaimed.

"Nah," Jeremiah shook his head in protest. "That was all Dr. Miami."

Brennon shook his head both at Jeremiah and his ringing phone, which he declined for the third time.

"She wants you to come back, huh?" Jeremiah asked.

"She's blowing me up." Brennon confirmed. "She's a fucking brat."

"We all know this, but she's your brat." Jeremiah shrugged it off. "So, why we acting like we don't already know what it is? You know gon leave the girl."

"I don't know…" Brennon ran his hand through his hair. "A muthafucka don't change after 11 years, it's because they're not going to."

"Would you even want her to, though? That's Storm. As much as we all love her, she can be a headache but that's your headache." Jeremiah reiterated. "That's the thing about marriage…. It's not gon be perfect…"

"Imagine the fuck out of that…" Brennon chuckled.

"The nigga that's not even married yet telling me about marriage."

"I'm just saying... You're either going to let it break you or make you. Some things you got to just let go. Divorce ain't even an option."

"Calm your ass down! Nobody's talking about no damn divorce. Damnn..." He laughed. "She gets mad at me all the time! I get mad one time, everybody acting like we getting a divorce."

"Alright while we wait for your ultrasound and blood work to come back let me ask you for more details." Dr. Smith sat down with her laptop in her lap ready to take notes. "Was this your first time feeling the stomach pains and shortness of breath?"

Storm shook her head. "Not with the stomach issues, that's been on and off a little while now. Some days I've felt completely fine, and others I can't even find a comfortable position to sleep in."

Dr. Smith nodded her head, still typing away at her keyboard.

"Also, I don't know if it's worth mentioning but... I've been having a lot of discomfort when it comes to sexual intercourse." Storm felt awkward even saying it.

"That is definitely worth mentioning. Is this during or after?" She questioned.

"Both. This is hella TMI..."

"No such thing."

"Whenever we've actually... finished it's been really painful for me afterwards and other time's it's been so painful that we couldn't."

Dr. Smith nodded her head and went through a series of questions. "Alright," she clasped her hands together. "We will get you those results back here soon and get you some answers."

"Thank you."

Holding onto her sister's hand, Storm was a combination of exhausted, nervous, and anxious.

"Good news." Camile stuck her head in the door. "Just got off the phone with Jeremiah, they're on the way. Also, your mama text me saying and I quote, answer your damn phone!"

"No!" Storm shook her head. "I don't want her rushing to get here any sooner. I'm okay.

"Alright..." When Dr. Smith returned, she wasn't alone, which already had Storm feeling like she was in trouble.

"I'm here... baby I'm here!" Brennon rushed into the hospital room and instantly went to Storm's side. He leaned in to kiss her on the forehead. "You okay?" He stroked the side of her cheek.

Storm nodded her head in response. She honestly didn't know, the doctor hadn't said yet, but him on her side gave her a new sense of relief.

"Alright, so… which do you want first- the good news or the bad news?" Dr. Smith asked.

There was bad news. Storm swallowed the lump in her throat.

"Just break it to me Doc." Storm replied dramatically.

"It really is a good thing you came in when you did. The bad news is that you are going to need to undergo emergency surgery…"

Storm gasped in panic as she squeezed Brennon's hand tighter.

"The good news is it's a fairly simple procedure. I promise you it sounds worse than it actually is." She explained. "Your body was trying to tell you something. Your ultrasound revealed there was a cyst about the size of a grapefruit that ruptured an ovary."

Storm's eyes grew big. She would make sure everyone else was good, but herself she would put on the back burner. She was terrible about checking on herself.

"The trouble you were having catching your breath was a result of something in your stomach being cut open by the rupture. We have to get on it ASAP to assess the damage to your ovary and also to stop the bleeding…"

Emergency surgery. Bleeding. Potential damage to her ovaries. Storm's head was spinning.

"That suffocating feeling you've been having while

trying to sleep is due to your diaphragm filling with blood." Dr. Smith continued.

Storm nodded her head; it was a lot of information, but she was taking every word of it in.

"The damage to my ovary... we're trying for our second baby." Storm expressed in a panic. "How will all of this effect that?" Her voice cracked.

"Again, that's something we have to look into with this surgery, but I will say this- there's still such a high percentage rate of women carrying successfully even if an ovary is to be removed, so I don't want you to worry, and I do want us to not jump the gun. Okay?"

Dr. Smith was trying her hardest to present her with the facts in the most straightforward way, but also keep her calm.

Storm was relieved, but not completely at ease. The tears that came flowing were solely from being overwhelmed. Slight fear, but mainly the overwhelming feeling that came from the abruptness of it all.

"Babe..." Brennon rubbed her arm gently. "Everything's going to be okay. I'm going to be right here." He kissed her on the forehead. "You're okay. You hear me?"

Storm nodded her head. He was no doctor, but for some reason when he said it, she felt and believed it.

***

The procedure took a little over an hour and a half.

Followed by a couple of hours of down time before Storm even woke up out of tiredness.

It was every bit of 5 in the morning.

The doctor had given Brennon the run-down of post-surgery protocol. He made mental notes of it all and Brennon had already determined she wouldn't be lifting a finger for the 6-weeks that the clamps were holding her stomach together.

Brennon's had already made up his mind that he'd been waiting on her hand and foot regardless.

"Oh noo… what are y'all still doing here?" Storm pointed. "I don't want everyone's night to be about me. This whole trip is about you Camile. I'm alright."

"Now you don't like everything being about you. Storm shut up." Kaice waved her off.

They could all laugh at her expense. Comic relief was always welcomed in their group.

"I had to know that you were okay sister, girl." Skully said, climbing in the hospital bed next to her sister.

"Skully." Storm whined. "This bed's barely big enough for me."

"You scared me to death." Skully replied.

"I couldn't tell. You laughed at me stupid." Storm pushed her half-heartedly.

"I didn't know, I thought you were pranking me or something."

"Bitch, I'm not a Youtuber, the hell? What'd you think it was a prank? A fucking drill?"

"I don't know! I was scared."

"Bitch so was I! I was on the ground!" Storm exclaimed.

They could laugh at it now, but at the moment it was terrifying.

"I think the scariest thing for me was how everything was just normal, and you were fine, and then you just weren't. You can't do me like that." Skully told her.

Storm let out a heavy sigh. "I really do appreciate y'all being here. Especially you Kaice, I know we're in this weird space right now. I know it's all my fault. I just don't know how to fix it."

Now wasn't the time or the place. "Just give it time, Storm." Kaice declared.

"Coffee anyone?" Wilma asked from the other side of the kitchen.

"Yes ma'am. Thank you." Kaice smiled.

"Where is this mystery date of yours, Kaice?" Camile asked curiously.

"He checked into a hotel." Kaice answered.

"Why?" Camile asked.

"I didn't want you to have to go out of your way to make any more room, and we're not in the stage of sleeping together so that wasn't happening." Kaice explained. "He's just fine."

They had a house full by that point. From grandparents to Camile's. Camile would give her that, but she also could tell she was trying to keep her situation a little more private. Camile would also give her that.

"Well, I can't wait to meet him."

"Maybe you already have."

"Oh, the suspense is just killing me."

They were mid conversation when Ariel came prancing into the kitchen.

Wilma did a double take, glasses touching the bridge of her nose. "Now look-a-here hoochie, I know you know your coochie is hanging out of those shorts." One thing Wilma was never going to do was bite her tongue.

For once Camile appreciated her outspokenness. Ariel being there still didn't sit right with her, but for the sake of keeping the drama to a minimum she wasn't harping on the issue.

"There's just no couth in walking around a house with mainly married men dressed like that." Wilma added.

"With all due respect, what reason does a married man have to be looking at me?"

"It's not about whether or not he would be looking, it's a respect thing."

"Don't expect her to get that." Kaice scuffed. "She doesn't even respect people's relationships."

That was one- line Kaice didn't cross, you had to be a different kind of scandalous to knowingly get involved with someone you knew was in a relationship.

"With all due respect, I show the same respect that people show to their own relationships." Ariel stated.

"Oh, listen at you!" Wilma quipped. "Talking that disrespectful shit like it's cute. Honey, let me fill you in on something I'm sure you've heard before. How you get him is how you lose him, if he doesn't respect the relationship he had with that girl for years what makes you think it's going to be any different with you? You've already shown him the type of woman you are. You can't think it's going to end any differently with you."

Ariel was stuck.

"I digress. We've all been young and dumb before."

"You smoking?" Brennon was shocked.

"Figured why not. I already feel good, might as well add to it." Jeremiah explained. "Something about marrying my best friend tomorrow got me on a natural high." He held out the blunt to Brennon.

They were recreational smokers at best if they felt like smoking- they smoked.

"That's a good thing you doing, J." Brennon inhaled the smoke, taking a couple more pulls before passing it back. "Camile's solid."

"I'm already knowing." Jeremiah agreed. "She's my best player on my team."

"I hear that."

"You know... I think that's why seeing you and Storm at odds bothers me so much. Y'all wedding was the first I had ever been to. Black love was always beautiful to me, but I never saw it in the family like that and you know society likes to glamorize all the wrong shit. Y'all the first ones that made this marriage shit seem coo to me."

Brennon nodded his head, exhaling as he passed the blunt. "I appreciate that. This health scare got me putting everything into perspective. It's like you said... I'm never leaving that girl. She's my whole world. Our little family is everything to me, so I'm just letting this small shit go. We put in too much work to get this solid. We breaking the hell out these cycles bruh."

"Agreed. Me and Camile been solid, to me these rings are just to let the world know what I been knowing, we locked in. I want the whole world to know!"

"The whole world, Cuz?" Brennon laughed, knowing his cousin was high as a kite and happy as a clam at high water.

"The whole world!" Jeremiah confirmed. "When you got somebody holding you down and fulfilling you in every way, why would you not go ahead and make it a for life thing? She deserves my loyalty for a lifetime."

"Damn, nigga you practicing your vows right now or something?"

Jeremiah laughed. "I'm just feeling good right now, man."

"Hey! Heyy!" A white man pointing his finger right at them with a hand on his hip called. "Hey!"

Jeremiah let the blunt out. If there was about to be a problem it could be that, but he'd prefer it not have to go there.

"Are you the owner?" He questioned.

"Huh?"

"Are you the fucking owner?!?"

Brennon and Jeremiah looked back and forth between one another.

"Nah."

"Tell them to trim their fucking hedges!" He yelled.

All Brennon and Jeremiah could do is bust out laughing.

"On that note, ima go take my shower and get back up to this hospital." Brennon stood to his feet. "That right there, just told me to leave that weed alone."

"If this trip gets any crazier." Jeremiah shook his head, still laughing.

The day was dedicated to fun. Camile had an array of activities planned for them on the beach.

They were buzzed just enough to be safe for water play.

They were having a blast on the jet skis, and parasailing; they all got on the banana boat as a group.

Law was first to fall off.

"I'm sorry baby, I don't do water." Skully didn't even offer a hand to him, she laughed as he swam his way back.

She was enjoying seeing him in a less serious matter, not taking himself or anything too seriously.

That was something she never got out of her last relationship.

Her ex was an angry person, with a lot of insecurities. Any scenario where he felt "embarrassed" became Skully's fault.

He would've fallen off that boat and Skully would have gotten her ass beat later for laughing. This was a level of ease she had never felt before.

Next to go was Ariel. "Another one bites the dust."

"She's a mermaid. She'll be aight." Camile shrugged it off.

"Nigga can't even swim to save his bitch." Jeremiah had joked.

They had all laughed it off, as Ariel utilized her floaties to make her way back.

15

*D*inner was ready just in time as the sun began to set. Everything from the view to the table décor was beautiful.

Their private chef and his team had done an excellent job.

"I just want to personally thank everyone for coming. Having the people who have supported and been a part of so many beautiful memories within this relationship, be a part of this wedding means the world to me. Ms. Wilma thank you for getting on that flight-even if it was against your will-" Camile chuckled, as well as some of the other family members who had witnessed Wilma's dramatic outburst about not wanting to fly.

"I love you all. With that being said, let's enjoy this good food and good champagne and enjoy this night because tomorrow I'm getting married!" She squealed.

For a minute there wasn't much talking going on, a telltale sign that the food was amazing, which it was.

There were still family members arriving late.

"Now you know I owe everyone an ass whooping." Treasure arrived loud and proud in her typical fashion. "For not telling me about my baby."

Skully got up to greet her mother. "We knew she would be okay ma, and we needed you to be. Couldn't have you having a conniption trying to get here."

"Yeah whatever. I should've been the first person called." Treasure wasn't happy about it.

"What we not gon do is start at this girl's dinner." Skully replied.

"No, what we not gon do is act like Ms. Treasure didn't come up in here showing up and showing out with this dress. And with this man." Camile looked to her side. "No RSVP. No heads up. Just another plus one. Don't nobody respect me here."

"Mama who is this man?"

"This is just my friend. Michael." She introduced nonchalantly with a shrug.

"Um huh. Michael, huh?"

"Well this is just great." Kaice clasped her hands together. "We can focus on Treasure's date and everyone can get off my back about mine."

"I heard there was a rehearsal dinner going on…"

"Nari!!!" Camile smiled walking over to greet her.

"For you and the hubby." Nari handed over the elegantly wrapped wedding gift.

Nari looked gorgeous in the emerald, green, floral satin dress with the cowl neckline and criss crossed back. Her hair was pulled up in a curly high ponytail and her makeup was flawless.

The girls surrounded her happy to see her.

"Hey Damitri." Skully greeted Nari's handsome date, her older brother.

He offered a head nod, as they shared a brief hug. Followed by a brief hug to Camile, and a lingering "something" with Kaice.

"Sorry I'm late."

"Forget late. We didn't know you were coming."

"I was always coming. I'm not missing the wedding regardless. I just needed to get my mind right." Nari clarified. "Where's my boo Storm?"

"The hospital. It's a story for another time, but she's alright." Skully explained.

She could feel him burning a hole through the side of her face, but she refused to give him anything.

"Well, come sit down. Get some food. A drink. You'll need a drink..." Camile muttered. "I've been trying to call you..."

"I know I've been purposefully hard to get in touch with, but we'll talk. Let me sit down and get my food though. I'm starving."

Damitri followed her lead. He was simply there

because he was asked to be. Having her brother there made Nari feel safe. Not just in the sense that she knew if Torrian jumped stupid Damitri would shut him down, but because she needed someone that was solely on her side.

It wasn't until she was seated with her plate, that she saw Torrian out of the corner of her eyes and noticed Ariel sitting beside him for the first time.

Her face must've worn her initial disgust because Kaice leaned in to speak to her, "You're okay, you're good. Don't even give him the satisfaction of a reaction."

Nari nodded her head, looking over at her brother, who wore a scowl. "It's okay."

Damitri was protective over her, as any big brother should be. With him it went a little deeper, because he'd always felt like more of a father figure.

So, when he saw his little sister hurt, he wanted to make other people hurt.

He had never been fully on board with the relationship, but he had schooled Nari so much that he'd felt she could handle herself. He would only step in when she deemed it necessary, which was why he was there with her.

Everyone was doing their best to avoid the elephant in the room. Conversation was flowing effortlessly.

Wilma was really carrying the dinner. From her stories about Jeremiah as a child, to her and Camile going back and forth with their sides of the story of when they were first introduced to one another.

It was smooth sailing until Nari excused herself to use the bathroom, the convenience of the beautiful house being right on the beach.

Nari was just walking out of the bathroom when she found herself face to face with Ariel.

"Sorry, didn't mean to scare you." Ariel apologized.

"You didn't." Nari stated flatly.

"Anyway…" Ariel cleared her throat. "I just didn't want you thinking me coming here was to spite you."

"Hm, so it wasn't."

"No. Torrian asked me to come as his date, and I know it's fucked up what happened between y'all but…"

"Do you hear yourself right now?" She could see Torrian walking up, but she still had something to get off her chest. "You're what happened to us, bitch! When would coming here after the role you played in the demise of my relationship not be spiteful? Are you dumb?"

"Aye," Torrian stepped in between them, urging Ariel to back up, and put some space between them. "She ain't got to be all that. Your beef is with me."

"You damn right it is, because I don't know that hoe from a can of paint, she doesn't owe me shit, but you! You wild." She shook her head. "You hurt me, and instead of doing what it takes to get me back, you choose to add salt to the wound."

"What do you call 200 missed phone calls? What do you call all this begging? I'm not even giving you the hell I could be giving you about kicking me out when I'm on the lease. I been keeping it playa giving you your space."

"Listen at you. You really think you doing something. You think that makes you an outstanding boyfriend? My bad, I got it all wrong. I should be thanking you for letting me kick you out after you disrespected me and our relationship." She said sarcastically. "Thank you so much for that Torrian."

"I don't even know why I'm trying." Torrian shook his head. "You already got your mind made up, and everything I say is a problem so…"

"This is how you try? This is your effort? Me having to sit across from the bitch you cheated on me with! After the way you've hurt me, why would you even put me through the pain of having to be in the same space as you and her together!"

"I only brought her here because I heard you were bringing a date."

The way that revelation cracked Ariel's face gave Nari a little satisfaction. She knew this already, and she was glad Ariel did too.

"The fact that you think that makes it any better shows how fucked up you are!"

"The fact that you're not even going to give us another chance, which shows...."

"Shows what?"

"It don't even matter." He threw up his hands. "You not tryna hear anything I have to say."

"Because you always got some dumb shit to say!" She shouted.

"And you always talking to me like you crazy!" He yelled back.

Nari let out an exasperated sigh. "I don't want to argue with you. I honestly don't even want to see you bruh. The fact that you thought you had the right to interrupt my peace, because you in your feelings! If I won't sit back and let you cheat on me in peace you won't let me have mine!"

"Come the fuck on, you hypin it now!" He dropped his head back like he was defeated. "I messed up one time, and you gon act like I haven't been nothing but a good nigga to you all these years."

"What does all the years matter when in the end you still turned around, and we did the one thing you know we can't come back from?" She stressed.

"Look I don't know what to do." He lowered his voice, and his head. "I'm losing my shit. I can't even play it coo. I never even stopped to think about the consequences of what life would be like without you."

"Now you don't have to think about it, you get to live it." She clasped her hands together. "Turned out to be exactly who I hoped you weren't."

"You already made me out to be the bad guy because that's who you wanted me to be. We were already destined for failure because I spent our whole relationship paying for the demons of your father."

"Wow, you really went there. People been telling me about you all along and it feels so good to really be able to see you for who you are right now. Keep going."

"I know you acting on anger and letting your friend get in your head. They been mad. Been wishing they had someone to even try to take care of them like me."

"Oh yeah, you think?" She chuckled bitterly. "You mean my friends who knew? You mean my friend whose cousin you're fucking!"

She could tell by the look on his face he actually thought he still had that little information under his belt. He didn't think she knew.

"You didn't even have the decency to not be sloppy." She shook her head.

Nor did he have the decency to give her a proper response. "So, you really gon let your pride make you lose a real nigga? Come on baby, I make my mistakes but you know what we had. I put up with a lot of shit Nari. I'm one of the good ones."

Camile entered the house, followed by Kaice. "I just wanted to make sure everything was good."

"The fact that you just said that to me. Whew." Nari shook her head in disbelief. "I swear once I heal from you, I'll never let you in the same way."

"You good?" That was her brother. He was now right beside her.

"We good." Nari confirmed. "Let's go."

But before they did, she had one last thing to get off her chest.

"Now the next time you want to come to me as a woman, don't." Nari stated blankly. Standing toe to toe with Ariel. "I've been sparing you sis. He owed me his loyalty, not you. I'll give you that, but at the end of the day you knew about me."

Some people's girl code didn't go beyond their personal group of friends, but Nari was simply a girls' girl.

"You were happy to be on the side, you were okay with hurting another woman. I guess now you think you got the one up, because he brought you here. Just know, you're something to do right now. You flew all this way just to have to witness him beg me to take him back, goofy. You're getting me off his mind sis."

"Either I'm lost." Nari started. "Or you are."

Nari was still emotional from the night before, but she wasn't hallucinating.

"How about neither?" Kaice smirked. "I think we're both exactly where we intended to be."

"Then I know why I'm here, but why are you in my

brother's hotel room?" Nari questioned and crossed her arms.

"She's a grown ass woman, she doesn't owe you an explanation." Damitri appeared from behind her carrying a tray of assorted breakfast foods.

"Excuse the hell out of me." Nari responded dramatically. "I just came to say I was dressed and ready when you are."

"Aw well, sit down and have some breakfast." Damitri insisted. "We'll head out in a little bit."

"So we just gon pretend like is just the norm. Okay." Nari nodded her head and found herself having the most awkward breakfast with her brother and Kaice.

———

The wedding had come together beautifully, while Camile was a minimalist- she was a perfectionist. She had put thought behind every single last detail of the wedding.

The white chiffon dual layer curtain was draped in yellow dahlia's- for commitment, white carnations- for good luck, yellow sunflowers for adoration, and white roses- for peace.

The chairs were lined with white roses and crystals. In each seat, there was a tropical themed wedding program fan, and a message in a bottle thank you favor.

Everything was beautiful.

Camile looked angelic. Her hair was swept to one

side by a beaded barrette, with her natural textured curls hanging to her shoulders.

Her ivory dress had a draped net bodice with pearl and crystal beading. Finished off with a crystal embroidery and a soft tulle ball gown bottom.

"You look gorgeous Camile." Storm smiled.

"Storm!" Camile squealed, walking over to her carefully holding her dress up to avoid dragging it. "How are you feeling?" She gave her a hug.

"Doesn't matter. It's not about me." Storm responded with a shrug. "How are you feeling?"

Camile relaxed a sharp exhale. "Excited. I'm ready!"

"Good. I just came back here to get you, because pops is out there looking sharp as a tack and Jelani's ready to kill her debut as flower girl so it's time for my good sis to walk down that aisle."

Everything flowed without a hitch.

The minute Jeremiah looked up and saw Camile standing at the end of the aisle next to her father, he couldn't compose the tears.

Brennon was right there patting his back.

His tears brought her to tears.

"Why are you crying baby?" He asked when she reached the end of the aisle.

"Because you're crying." Camile chuckled.

This brought a quiet laughter to the audience who watched the sweet moment between the couple, as he attempted to help save her makeup.

"Okay, okay." Camile fanned her face. "We're good."

The tears were like a chain reaction. From the pastor, to Camile and Jeremiah's beautiful vows to one another.

Simply put, the wedding was amazing.

The reception was everything. They got a ten out of ten for the three things that matter the most: décor, food, and the DJ.

Camile and Jeremiah were seafood lovers, so the menu was a seafood lover's dream.

The menu consisted of Lobster tails, salmon, seafood potato salad, lobster mac and cheese, a pasta dish, mussels, three-cheese oysters, filet mignon and bacon wrapped asparagus.

The food was buffet style, and the alcohol was open bar.

Anyone who wasn't on the dance floor was either eating or getting a refill.

"Hey, can we talk?" Kaice asked.

"Go ahead." Nari replied.

"I'll give y'all a minute." Storm stepped back.

"You're good." Nari told her.

"Well, I just wanted to clarify some things about me and your brother. Don't want you thinking I was trying to do anything behind your back."

"You mean like how you were?" Nari crossed her arms. "After everything I've been going through you think I really want to have to question another one of my friends? My brother though Kaice?"

Kaice let out a heavy sigh. She wasn't usually the type to explain herself, so she was already going out of her way to even make Nari comfortable with the situation.

She could understand her having reservations, but she couldn't tolerate disrespect.

"I'm playing." Nari laughed. "Girl, I don't care. Just don't play with my brother because I'm not playing bout him."

"Me either, so that makes two of us." Kaice grinned.

"Oh Lord," Nari shook her head, with a chuckle. "Y'all have met y'all match in each other I can tell you that, but I'm not letting y'all get on my nerves. I'm still confused as to how this even happened."

"Well…"

"No-no-no. Just spare me the details."

"Don't spare me! I want all the tea." Storm had to stop herself. "My bad I got a little beside myself, I forgot we not there yet."

"Right."

Storm and Kaice had always been the type of friends that told each other- everything. That hurt a little.

"Girl you know ima call you later." Kaice stuck out her tongue as they slapped hands.

"What'd I miss over here?" Skully walked over.

"Kaice and Damitri."

"Good for you Kaice, done lucked up and got you a real one."

"What??" Nari gawked. "Let me find out all we had to do was get Skully a man for her not to be so mean."

"I told y'all all sis needed was a little hard peen." Kaice teased.

"You know what..." Skully walked away giving them all her middle finger.

———

"Never known you to be a wallflower." Storm sat down next to Torrian. "Where's your girl?"

"Don't start with me, Storm. I'm not on that." He shook his head.

He had sent Ariel home and was left to sulk. While everyone, Nari especially, seemed to be living their best lives.

All she had to do was follow his eyes that were fixed on Nari, to know what he was on. He wore his regret all over his face.

"Boy nobody's trying to start with you." Storm rolled her eyes. "Contrary to what you like to believe, I was rooting for y'all. Seeing lil sis happy came before any of the little petty back -and- forth shit we do. Besides that, I know you're not a bad person."

"Yeah right."

"I mean it. I think you're a man- a young man and

as bad as you want to say, if you could take it all back you would. You wouldn't."

"Fuck outta here. So, you're telling me knowing what I know now, I would cheat again and lose my girl?"

"Yes, because no matter how you flip the dice, you can't look me in my eyes and tell me you never thought Nari leaving you was a consequence of you cheating. You just thought you wouldn't get caught. So, I believe if you could do it all again you just wouldn't get caught because you can't admit the real truth."

"What's that?" He kissed his teeth out of irritation. "Since you just know everything."

"You're not ready to be tied down right now, because even in that honesty you could still end up losing her. Which isn't an option because it's not that you don't want her... it's just that you can't be the man she needs you to be for her right now. Doesn't make you a bad guy. Doesn't mean you can't ever be but admitting that comes with risk that you weren't ready to face so you did the worst thing you could possibly do."

Admitting she was right was the hardest thing he could do, but she was truly like that big sister that he could never get along with but had love for.

"Men and women look at cheating in different ways, men can cheat without even blinking. We for the most part equate sex with feelings. That in combination with the fact that it was just the one girl, and not just one time. You basically started a whole new relationship, and you didn't do yourself any favors by bringing her to this wedding."

"It wasn't even like that."

"To her it was exactly like that. To any woman it was exactly like that. You just opened a whole world of insecurities for that girl."

He ran his hands over his face, shaking his head. "Lost a good thing."

"Or learned a good lesson." Storm retorted.

"Now that I've learned my lesson, how do I fix it?"

"Torrian." She pat him on the shoulder as she stood to her feet. "Learn the lesson first."

"She's pretty when she tries, huh?" Storm had spotted Law admiring Skully from the afar.

"She's beautiful when she doesn't." Law corrected her.

The response warmed Storm's heart like it was geared towards her. To know that her sister was being loved in the right way was fulfilling in every way.

"You know... I love that girl to death." Storm stated. "She's literally my other fucking half and when he who shall remained unnamed, took her through the hell that he did... I felt every bit of it. It felt worse being so hopeless when someone I loved was being hurt so badly. But she loved him, so what could I really do?"

Law nodded his head. He empathized with her because he could relate.

Even in situations where there was nothing he could do, he felt so strongly for the people he cared about that he wore that burden.

"The Skully you see today... the woman she's becoming- who I am so proud of..." She smiled as her voice cracked on her next words. "She's so strong now because she was so weak then. She's put herself together, only after being completely broken down. I will never see my sister that low again, you hear me?"

"You never will. Not by my doing."

Storm nodded her head. "I believe that. I believe you won't hurt her in that way, and I believe she won't allow it. If I haven't made it clear already, I'm not playing about her. Ever."

"You have. I've seen your bad side I don't think I want to be on it."

"Hey. You treat her right, I'll treat you better. I am my sister's keeper."

"See now when you say shit like that, combined with that look in your eye... I can't lie... I'm a little scared."

"You should be." They both laughed.

Her sister was in a much better place.

She had a lot of people that cared for her and Law a welcomed addition to the list.

"Welcome to the family Law." She patted him on the back."

———

"Oh, cut this off. Boring me to tears with these love songs." Nari yawned. "Play something for the single girls."

"Chill out Ne-Yo. All of a sudden you so sick of love songs." Skully teased.

They still had the Airbnb for that night, so even though Camile and Jeremiah had left for their honeymoon right after the reception they had one last night to party.

Nari pushed her playfully.

"You think this is heartbreak then you better saddle up youngin." Treasure shook her head. "You're going to be taken on the best rides of your life by men. You're going to be taken on the worst rides of your life by men, but the ride… the ride will always be worth it. "Why do you think we put up with these men and their shit?"

"Why do you think they put up with ours?" Storm added. "I mean after all my recent bullshit ima have to saddle up."

"Well, you better be careful, you know that stomach is barely holding together right now."

"I know," Storm sighed, not even wanting to think about the surgery scar on her stomach or the clamps holding her stomach together. "Six weeks. Then ima *rideee til I can't no more.*"

"That shouldn't take too long." Kaice quipped.

"Word on the streets is you can't ride no more so…"

Storm couldn't even be mad at Kaice for getting her joke off, or the laughter that followed.

"What am I missing?" Treasure looked around confused.

"Nothing you need to know anything about ma…" Storm shook her head.

"Anyway, we bout to go for a ride." Skully said standing to her feet.

"Um huh I bet." Storm smirked.

"Later!"

"Now… I ain't but two seconds off you." Storm turned to her mother. "Showing up with Mr. Michael all salt and pepper bearded. Looks like you were doing some riding yourself."

"Where's my belt?"

"I'll hold her down for you!" Kaice volunteered. "Beat her ass ma!"

"Go to sleep, Babe." Brennon insisted, he stroked her head that lay across his chest.

"I can't sleep. I don't want to, anyway." Storm replied. "I want to talk to my husband. I don't want this to be another issue we sweep under the rug."

"Shits dead, Storm." Brennon stated. "All I care about is my wife being okay."

"All I care about is us being okay." She lifted her

head, turning to look him in the eyes. "I need you to know that I do respect you."

"I know this. You think I would still be with you if I didn't…"

"I know it's just, when I listen to the way your brother thinks…"

"That's where I have to stop you, Torrian is that lil brother that you love to death, but you have to slap up sometimes. You certainly don't listen to him."

"He's not all wrong, though. My actions don't always show it, but I have the utmost respect for you as a man, as a husband. Brennon I really am sorry. I love you so much, and I appreciate you for the amazing man that you are. You are my everything, and I take it for granted all the time because I'm so used to you always being here, I never even considered what it would be like if you weren't."

It shocked him that she even thought like that, because in his heart he knew he was never going anywhere.

There wasn't anything that Storm could do that would convince him there was anyone else out there for him. All their problems felt worth working through. He could even find the good in her flaws. Six- years before when he proposed and decided she was who he wanted to spend the rest of his life with he felt what he felt now which was that Storm was his end-all-be-all.

"Everyone knows you're too good for me, including

me." Storm continued. "I'm always on the defense wondering when you're going to realize I'm not even worth the headache and leave me. Baby please don't give up on me."

"I would never. I could never. Stop questioning something that's a sure thing. Quit looking for the wrongs in something that's so right. We're locked in for life." He lifted her hand to his lips kissing it. "I love you Storm."

"Even though I'm so hard to love? Why do you even put up with my shit?"

"That's not even the case. You're so easy to love, just hard to manage but the challenge is part of what I fell in love with. It'd be silly of me to not expect it at this point. I'll always love you, and ima always put up with your shit."

"I'm about to ugly cry right now." Storm used her free hand to fan her eyes.

"You a lil ugly anyway." He teased. They laughed together.

"You think everyone's getting along?" Camile wondered. They were on their flight to Aruba.

"I'll be honest, I don't give a damn how them people doing." Jeremiah shrugged nonchalantly. "They just better leave that AIRBNB in one piece."

Camile laughed as he looked over at her. "You're so beautiful Cam. My beautiful ass wife!"

"Wife." Camile repeated. "That hit different. I mean I was a bomb ass girlfriend. A phenomenal fiancé. I promise you I'm about to be a hell of a wife."

16

2-Weeks-Later

"*I*'m surprised you called." Torrian stated.

"We have things to talk about. Nari shrugged.

"I agree." Torrian nodded his head.

"Not about what you think though." Nari assured him.

They hadn't been in contact since the wedding.

Which had probably been harder for him then her, but he had decided to take Storm's advice.

"I gave a lot of things some thought, and what you said was true. I wasn't being fair by putting you out of a place that we shared…"

"So, you're letting me move back in?"

"Yeah. If you want it's all yours. I'm moving out."

The color drained from his face. The excitement

he'd mustered from the little bit of hope he'd gotten was gone just like that.

"You serious right now?"

"As a heart attack. What did you think Torrian? That I was going to just cool off and everything would go back to normal?"

"I been really respectful of your space and giving you your time…"

"You're respecting my space, but you couldn't even respect our relationship? How does that sound Torrian?!?" She yelled getting closer to his face. "I never needed to cool off! I needed my boyfriend to be loyal to me! You don't respect me!"

"When have I ever disrespected you?!?"

"When you cheated on me!!! What type of bitch do you really think that I am Torrian?" She took her hand right across his face.

"Bruh." He took a hold of her wrist. "Stop putting your hands on me!"

"Get off of me." She pushed him away. She ran her hands through her hair. It annoyed her that she allowed him to get a rise out of her every time. She was breathing heavily and visibly flustered.

"Listen, I didn't call you over to argue. I called because I'm moving. I already talked to the Landlord. You can stay here if you choose to, and if not, and we have to break the lease, I'm willing to pay the fee. So, what's it gonna be?"

A moment of silence passed between them.

Reality was setting in, she wasn't bulging. Once she moved out that was that. The fact that he could still get this much emotion out of her let him know the feelings were still there, but that didn't make him feel good.

"We really bringing the worst out of each other." He shook his head, taking a seat on the couch. He buried his face in his hands before looking up at her.

Nari cleared her throat. "I shouldn't have put my hands on you. Before or now. I got out of character. That was wrong, and I'm sorry for that. It was just so hard to not want to lay your ass out in that moment, and now."

Torrian chuckled. They had shared so many moments, good and bad. This moment was bringing them closer to closure, which signified the closing of their relationship, and that was a hard pill to swallow. It was his fault, and he knew it.

"I ruined our relationship. I know what I had, and I don't want anyone else to have it, but I blew it. Now I have to accept that because I don't want to ruin you."

In all honesty, Nari believed that he was remorseful but still didn't think he realized the damage he had already done. Moving forward, Nari knew she would move differently in her next relationship.

"Wouldn't even feel right staying here without you. I'll pay whatever fee. Just tell me when we got to be out."

"Thank you." She said softly.

"I really am sorry, Nari. You're my first love, ima always have you for you."

Nari only nodded her head as he leaned in for a hug. "Nah," She shook her head. "Too soon Torrian. Too soon."

"What about a kiss?"

"See, this is why I get violent. Fuck outta here!"

"I'm just glad to see you laughing, man. I didn't think there was going to be a time when we'd be in the same room again without you wanting to run up on me."

"Well... I been working on me. Got this wine and woosah thing going on. Don't get me wrong, I would still like to beat your ass."

"On that note, ima head out."

"As you should."

Torrian laughed, stepping back. He was glad to see her laughing, grateful for any glimmer of hope.

———

"I'm glad we could get out like old times today." Storm smiled. "I missed you, girl."

They'd met for brunch, that started off a little awkward but 4 mimosas later they were back to normal.

"I mean, of course. I'm Kaice." She boasted.

Storm chuckled, shaking her head. "For real though, you've been the best friend to me. Whether I've deserved it or not. Never changed up. All of this has made me realize I got to tighten up. I'm afraid if I don't take the time to change some things about myself, I could lose the people that matter to me the most."

"You mean you're not perfect Storm?" Kaice said sarcastically.

"Surprising, right?"

"I'm giving you a hard time, but I can admit I might've overstepped my boundaries sometimes."

"You don't say? Like maybe when you snitched on me to my husband?"

They could both laugh at that. Neither of them was serious about the shots that they were taking at each other.

"I think I just felt so lonely at times. Y'all have been like the only real family I have because you know how rocky everything is with my own. Being around y'all makes me feel good. Feels like what a real family is supposed to feel like."

"Okay stop." Storm fanned her eyes, "You're going to make me cry."

"I just love all of y'all so much. Even Skully's ass. I wasn't trying to overstep anything with Brennon, he's just a really good guy as you know and it's easy to talk to him. Helped me realize I kept giving my all to relationships that didn't benefit me any."

"Just forget these good lashes and mascara then!" Storm threw her hands up. "It was never about you and Brennon. All about me and the insecurities I was dealing with. I would never come in between y'all friendship. Everybody deserves a little Brennon in their life, and I have the best part- his heart. I got to do better by that."

"We all got some things to work on, and ima need you to work on that mouth ma'am."

"It's lethal, huh?"

"It is, and the next time you come at me the way you did-" Kaice pointed her finger right at her. "You gon have to shoot me my round."

"I've text you a couple times." Tatum stated firmly.

Tatum had come dressed to entice.

Her hair was pulled up into a pineapple hairstyle, with her curls cascading down the sides of her face, and wore a minimal makeup look with mascara and a red lip.

Dressed in a black bodysuit that served her cleavage on a platter, black high-waisted jeans, and a pair of black booties. The simplest look that she absolutely bodied.

"I saw." Law confirmed.

"We ignore each other now?" Tatum questioned. "One thing I don't do is beg, you realize how crazy you got me looking?"

"Sorry you feel that way. I just been chilling."

"I hope you don't mind me ordering without you. I did get us some appetizers. Fried pickles, I'm starving."

"I'm not. This shouldn't take long anyway. What's up Tatum?"

"It's like that?"

The waitress came back offering Law a menu and something else by her demeanor. She was doing a little too much for Tatum's liking. "He's good. I'm good. Thank you." She forced a smile.

She gave Law one last smile, before rolling her eyes to Tatum and walking away.

"Look, before anything else we've always been friends... A lot more than that too, but I guess you're too wrapped up in little miss tattoo barbie to care about anyone else's feelings."

"See, this is what I don't have time for Tatum."

"Make time!" Her voice rose a few octaves. "You think after all these years I'm just bout to let you play me to the left? You really think that's a good look for you? With all those tacky ass tattoos..."

"Sorry I'm late." Skully walked over to the table like her presence was anticipated. She gave Law a quick kiss before taking the seat to his right which put her right in between the two of them.

She took her time removing her jacket, all the while Tatum sat there seething.

"Wow. You had to follow your man because you can't trust him alone with me? Afraid he might come to his senses?" Tatum accused. "Shows how insecure you are."

"I didn't have to follow him anywhere. He invited me." Skully shot a glare in Tatum's direction. "What'd I miss?"

The two women were having a stare down.

"Look I'm not trying to get in the middle of this female shit." Law cleared his throat. "Tatum, I've had a lot of love for you over the years. In our friendship and in our relationship. Now I need you to give that respect to my new relationship. I care about this girl and this is who I'm with. If you can't respect her and our relationship, it's a done deal."

"No, it is a done deal." Skully corrected. There weren't any ifs to it as far as she was concerned.

Tatum was going to keep crossing the line because she thought she could.

Years of dealing with Law on and off had her thinking she had ties to him forever, which wasn't the case. Skully didn't share.

"All that friendship shit is dead." Skully stated blankly.

She hadn't even spoken to Law about it. That was just that. Those were one of her non-negotiables. It wasn't the fact of him having female friends, but this female friend was a no.

"You can't tell him who he can and can't be friends with."

"But I can. I won't allow it. Not if he wants to be

with me. You see I never would've had a problem with you. It's always you with the slick comments and the funky ass attitude you've had with me since day one. It's clear you'll never have respect for me or for the boundaries of my relationship. Probably any relationship of Law's if you're not in it. So," She clasped her hands together to finalize her statement. "You've lost those privileges."

"You're just letting her speak for you now Law?" Tatum's eyes darted to him.

Skully turned her attention to him as well.

"I said what I had to say." He shrugged. "All the extra cattiness is between y'all. That's my girl. I got to back her. Sorry Tatum. I got love for you, but it is what it is."

Skully revealed a satisfied smile. "You ready?" She turned to him.

She was confident that this was the last of the Tatum drama. Law was giving his word- she trusted that and wasn't giving the situation any more life.

Later that night Skully and Law were enjoying the dinner of pepper steak, rice, and peas that she had prepared.

"Tell me all about the internship." Skully insisted. "I want to know how it's going."

"So far, so good." Law answered. "Mr. Dixon really looked out. I've been in other settings where people's only interest has been in making sure I don't surpass them."

"That's what's up." Skully nodded her head. "That's a fact. People hate to see you doing better than them. It's like that in every field and it really is sad."

"Too many people out here with that crab in a bucket mentality." Law shook his head. "So many more of our people could be thriving if we looked out for each other."

When she felt her cell phone vibrating on the table caught her attention. "Give me a second, I have to take this." She excused herself from the table.

Law wasn't necessarily eavesdropping, but the bits and pieces of the conversation he did overhear had him curious.

"Yes!" She exclaimed on her way back to the table. She took a seat back across from him and took a sip of her drink with a smile on her face.

"What's up?" He asked. "What we celebrating?"

After taking another sip from her drink she answered, "I got approved for the apartment I wanted."

He knew that she had struggled a bit with finding an apartment that checked off all her boxes and would approve her had been challenged since the eviction bomb got dropped on her.

What he didn't know was that she had even been looking still.

"I didn't even know there was an apartment that

you wanted." He replied. "Sounds like good news for you and bad news for me."

"How you figure?" She asked, eyebrows furrowed in confusion.

"Are you trying to tell me something?"

"No, not at all."

"You trying to get away from me? I can't be worse than your last roommate." He joked.

"No. Not at all." She shook her head. "I think we're heading in the right direction. The Skully you get today is after working through the damage of being hurt by someone you've let close enough to hurt you. I'm much different than that person I was years ago, but I've still got some working on myself to do. I think we have the potential to be something great, in whatever entity that is for us."

"I just think the only way we stand a chance is if we slow this shit down now. That way you don't go disappearing on me for a couple days at a time again." She threw a joke in there.

Law chucked. "Alright I deserve that."

"Do you understand what I'm trying to say?"

"I overstand." Law nodded his head.

He wanted them to work too. He didn't have any intentions in dropping the ball like he did before, but he could respect her reservations since he had.

"I can't even lie though your presence will be missed around the house. You still gon come over and cook for me?"

"Oh that's all you gon miss my cooking?"

"Don't flatter yourself now, because that macaroni ain't hitting on much."

Skully's mouth dropped open. "Wow. It's like that?"

"Well, you're moving out so... I'm a little bitter."

Skully couldn't recall ever feeling the things that she felt for Law. Though she wouldn't say she was in love just yet, she had gained a trust in him, which meant so much more.

Everything about the way he handled her let her know they were on the right track.

"Don't be." Skully smiled. "I'm not going anywhere. There's no getting rid of me."

Skully was happy with the space they were in.

With the past behind her she was happy to have something to look forward to.

"You know what I'm going to miss the most?" She grinned.

"What's that?"

"That chair."

"The chair?"

Skully nodded her head. "It holds... a special memory."

"Hm, you might have to jog my memory."

She stood from her chair and repositioned herself in his lap. "Just don't let me fall this time."

EPILOGUE

"Thank y'all for coming over to help me move." Nari exclaimed. "I don't think y'all know how crazy it was making me just being in that house."

Nari had moved across the bridge with her brother to Indiana. 10-to-15-minute drive, 20 with traffic.

It was temporary, but Nari had also felt it was for the best.

"Yeah, yeah. Of course." Skully nodded her head. "Now I know I got some movers locked in for when I move."

"If you and Law are doing good, why exactly are you moving out?" Storm crossed her arms. "Explain that to me again."

"Ugh-no. Long as the person that matters understands I'm not explaining it to nobody else." Skully replied.

"Still struggling with the whole mind your business thing, huh Storm?" Camile commented.

"You know what… Ima just shut up, but one day y'all gon want me in y'all business and I'm not gon have nothing to say."

"Yeah, don't count on it."

"For real, I really do appreciate y'all. I've been really angry and bitter, and it's been hard not to lose myself to the hurt of it all, but each of you has played a role in keeping me afloat. Like the sister's I never had." Nari continued. "Storm, you're like my partner in crime. Camile, you're like the voice of reason even though no one listens." They all laughed as she went around the circle. "Kaice, you're the lover, you're so tough but fragile at the same time. You're just a real one…"

"And your potential in-law." Kaice joked. "Don't forget that."

"Relax. Chill out." Nari replied. "Skully you… you're… Still trying to figure you out, because sometimes I just don't know if you like any of us. Still got love for you though.

"I think I'm speaking for all of us when I say you're like the baby sister of the crew, and we're all here if you need us."

"Yes, and as someone who has been through some traumatizing things in a relationship I just want to say- it's going to hurt and even when you think the hurt is over it's going to show up a little bit in your relationships that follow. Even when you don't realize it." Skully was opening up, something she rarely did. Talking about her past relationship, something she never did.

"Just don't let anyone tell you what is traumatic for you, or how long it takes you to get over that. Because it's a lot of hurt people, out here hurting people, because they can't acknowledge their own pain." Skully added.

"All that!" Kaice backed her up. "As women we're always told we're too emotional, and too often our feelings are disregarded. Whole time we really warriors and some of these men not even equipped to handle everything we handle. And still look good."

"Say that, say that!" Nari nodded her head.

"But shout out to the real ones that do hold it down." Storm interjected. "My husband the shit."

"I got a good one too, but I still feel for y'all." Camile said.

"Alrighttt. We got the moving out the way, whatever that mushy shit was just now, now let's get some shots!"

They traveled down to the kitchen. Where Nari poured them each a shout of Patron.

"Alright everyone propose a toast." Nari insisted holding up her glass. "To my sisters, from another mister."

"To fresh starts, and open hearts." Skully lifted her glass.

"To loving and putting ourselves first." Kaice added her statement.

"To us, the wonderful men behind us, and the amazing men who will find us." Camile added on the latter for the single ladies.

"And to my Nari boo…" Storm smiled. *"You is smart. You is kind. You is important."* She spoked the movie line. "That's word to Celie nem."

They all laughed as they downed the clear liquor. That would probably be a long-lasting insider from the game night.

"Y'all just gon turn my little bachelor's pad right out, huh?" Damitri commented, entering the kitchen.

He'd just gotten off work, and was so used to having his alone time, the commotion in the kitchen almost caught him off guard.

"Bachelor's pad, huh?" Kaice commented. They made some type of lustful eye contact that Nari had to look away from.

"Hey ladies." He greeted them, retrieving water from the refrigerator. "Kaice…"

"Oh, we just the ladies and Kaice, huh?" Nari shook her head.

"Hello, Nari. My spoiled lil baby." Damitri pulled her into a hug. Kissing her on the cheek.

"Alright, enough." Nari whined. "Get off me."

"Alright, alright. Pour us another shot…" Camile directed. "Damitri, join us."

"I was going to say, just help yourself to all my liquor." Damitri teased.

"We're going to have another round, and then we're going to all go get dressed because we're going out." Camile exclaimed. "Y'all owe me. The bachelorette party that never was."

"Is that who I think it is?" Kaice pointed.

All their eyes zeroed in on Ebony in an ill fitting one piece, and a part-less wig.

Damitri was the only one in the dark. He was still trying to figure out how Kaice had trapped him into going out with all females.

Storm downed the remainder of her martini, down to the olive. She hated olives.

As good of a time as they were having, Skully couldn't even wrap her head around the reasons why Kaice would point her out. But like her sister she was steaming.

"Ladies, let us remember we've all been working on our zin." Nari stated. "Remember! Wine and woosah." She nudged Camile for backup.

"Yes!! Wine and woosah." Camile encouraged with a little breathing exercise.

"I don't really fuck with wine like that." Storm stated standing to her feet just as Skully did the same.

"Me either." Skully shook her head.

"Remember you're still in the cathouse Storm. Do you really think Brennon wants you out here fighting?"

"The clamps sis!" Nari reminded her. "The clamps!"

Skully was already crossing the room.

"Call Law school!" Storm called over her shoulder following behind her sister.

SYNOPSIS:

Skully, Storm, Camile, Nari, and Kaice are all in different phases of their lives and relationships.

While Skully has deemed love a losing game, her twin Storm seems to have a perfect marriage. However, everything isn't always as it seems, and love is always in the air whether Skully finds herself ready for it or not.

Kaice- the hopeless romantic, who is not lacking in partners just the romantics is watching all her friends fall in love, and slowly rethinking her prior love choices.

Nari is young and in love but refuses to be young and dumb. Which may come at a price, some of her defenses may cost her the same love she's fighting for.

Meanwhile, Camile is experiencing the happiest time of her life and trying to keep everyone from falling apart simultaneously.

Even as their friendships and love get tested, they're determined to not only get through it, but get through it together and not get caught in the trauma and confusion of it all.